Crayford Hall

5 - 11. 10

Robert A Lane

TO NURSE MAGGIE
THIS IS MY NEW BOOT
HOPE YOU LIKE IT

Rol

Pen Press

YOUR
FRIEND
ROBERT LANE.

First published in Great Britain by Pen Press

All paper used in the printing of this book has been made from wood grown in managed, sustainable forests.

ISBN13: 978-1-907499-64-7

Printed and bound in the UK
Pen Press is an imprint of Indepenpress Publishing Limited
25 Eastern Place
Brighton
BN2 1GJ

A catalogue record of this book is available from the British Library

Cover design by Jacqueline Abromeit

I would like to dedicate this book to Janet

Thank you for all your help
In making this book
Possible

About the Author

Robert A Lane was born in west London.
After serving in the army and merchant navy he spent most of
his life in transport.

His hobbies include martial arts, playing the guitar, writing short
stories and poetry.

He currently lives in Hornchurch Essex with his wife Janet.

Contents

And One Is Two

Margaret Ann Wilson rang her younger sister Pat to make arrangements to meet the next day in their local shopping mall for coffee and to do some shopping. After talking for some time Pat said, "I've got to go; the children have just come in. Bye, see you tomorrow!" and with that she put the phone down.

As soon as she put the phone down it rang, thinking it was her sister she picked it up and said, "What have you forgotten this time?"

But the voice said, "Is that Margaret Ann Wilson?"

"Yes, who is it?" Then as if something invisible was trying to pull or suck something out of her throat hard and fast it was coming out of her throat into the telephone. And at the same time her arm holding the phone was locked, she could not move her arm. Her mouth was fixed open as though she had lockjaw, her chest went very tight then the phone went dead. She could move her arm okay again and she could close her mouth as normal and the pain in her chest went.

She put down the phone and sat down. Whatever had just happened to her had scared the life out of her, she was shaking and sat there for over an hour, before making herself a cup of tea. It was now getting on late afternoon and she was back to her old self. She heard her husband come in and went to say hello to him but found she could not talk – only whisper.

"Are you alright darling?" asked her husband.

"Fine, I've got a bit of a sore throat."

"Oh, I'll get you something for it."

But the next morning her voice was back and she felt okay, and life was back to normal as before the phone call. It was about five weeks later when Margaret had almost forgotten about the call and she had just got back home from shopping when the phone rang, she picked it up and a voice said, "Is that Margaret Ann Wilson?"

"Yes, who is this please?"

"I am your own voice, listen, do you not recognise your own voice?"

"Who is this please?"

"I just told you I am your voice!" At that she slammed down the phone. Ten minutes later the phone rang again and Margaret just sat and looked at it, she picked it up and it was her husband, "Just letting you know I'll be home about five, see you later" and he was gone. Again when John came home she never said a word about the phone call.

A few days later the phone rang again, "Hello Margaret," the voice said, "Don't hang up, I've got to talk to you."

"Is this a joke or something?"

"No, no joke, listen to my voice is it not yours?"

"Er yes it sounds like me. What do you want?"

"I want to warn you of danger."

"What danger?"

"You plan to get the bus tomorrow to go shopping – don't take it, for it will crash and many people will get badly hurt!"

"But there are a lot of buses going to town tomorrow."

"I'm talking about bus 155 from Tines Corner at eight in the morning."

"How do I know you are telling the truth?"

"I will prove it to you, I will tell you about yourself. You were born on the 27th August 1960 at St Peter's Hospital."

"Everyone knows that."

"Okay only you know this, you had your first love affair in Trampton Country Park with Billy Mayford."

"Billy could have told you that!"

"Last Friday at 11 o'clock in the morning you felt sick, dizzy and had a bad headache and lay down on your bed until 2 o'clock. You were the only person in your house at the time. Am I right?"

"Yes, but how did you know that?"

"I told you I am your voice. So you want more?"

"Yes,"

"Our mother's photo – you have it in your wallet, no one knows you have that photo."

"What do you mean 'our mother'?"

"I told you I am your voice, remember do not ride the bus. Just one more thing to prove who I am, when I first rang you your arm was locked and your mouth was too, also you had pain in your chest and your throat. You remember?"

"Yes I do."

"Good, I must go" and with that the phone went dead.

"Am I dreaming this? It can't be real." But deep down she knew it was real. John did not come home a happy man, "Damn car is playing up I had to get Tom to drop me off. I think I'll get rid of it, now I'll have to go to work by bus tomorrow."

"Which bus?" Margaret asked him.

"The 155 from Times Corner" Margaret went cold.

"Oh God!" She said to herself.

"Are you alright?"

"Yes fine just a little bit tied today. I've been thinking you know, you have a days' holiday to come and you've got to used it up?"

"Yes…"

"Well why don't you have tomorrow off and we can walk over to Brain and Sue's and see their new baby. We haven't been over yet"

"Yes that's a good idea. I'll ring up to see if it's okay." A few minutes later he came back "Yes I can have tomorrow off." With that she gave him a big hug and said to herself, "Thank you Lord!"

At 11 o'clock the next day they left their house and got to Brain and Sue's at 11.50am, "Hi nice to see you both" Brain said. After seeing their new baby, Amy, he said, "Did you hear about the accident this morning ?"

"No what accident?" "

The 155 from Times Corner ploughed into the bakers and they said the driver had a heart attack. A lot of people got hurt, some are in a bad way."

"Oh dear was anybody killed?"

"No but from what I can hear they were very lucky"

"What time did it happen?"

"It was 8 o'clock."

"Oh," Margaret said.

John looked at her and said, "I would have been on that bus if you hadn't said about popping over to see Brain and Sue's baby!" Margaret just closed her eyes. For the next few weeks life got back to normal again, no voice phone calls, just family and friends.

It was just after John had gone to work that the phone rang, thinking it was John who had forgotten something Margaret picked up the phone and said, "What have you forgotten this time, your head?"

But the voice said, "Listen Margaret, it's me your voice. Your friends are in danger, ring Brain and Sue and tell them not to light the gas fire; if they do it will explode and they could get killed or badly injured. Do it right away!" the phone went dead. "Oh God not again!"

She rang Brain but he did not answer, "Answer for God's sake, answer!" but it rang and rang, "Answer, please answer," then a voice said "Hello?"

"Is that you Brain?"

"Yes"

"It's Margaret, listen – don't light your gas fire. Don't light it, please listen. Ring the gas board right away, tell them it's an emergency."

"What's going on Margaret?"

"Just do what I say, don't light it okay?"

"Okay,"

"Brian do what I say, ring them and ring me back as soon as you have rang them."

For nearly five minutes she stood by the phone, "Come on ring back, ring back!"

Then it did ring, "The gas board are on their way, thank God Sue and the baby are out of the house. I have to go."

"After they have been, ring me"

"I will, I'll tell you later." It was nearly two hours later that the phone rang, "I don't know how you knew but if I had lit the fire we would all be dead, there was a bad gas leak under the floor boards, the house would have been a pile of rubble and we would have been under it. Thanks, I don't know how you knew but you saved our lives. Thank you!"

"Thank God you're all safe."

"We are thanks to you! The gas board told me if I had clicked the ignition button the spark would have blown us up and probably the houses either side of us."

"What did they do?"

"Put all new pipes in. It's okay now, Sue said 'thanks'."

"As long as you are okay that's all that matters. I'll see you later." Margaret put the phone down. Brain and Sue came round that night and said, "I don't know how you knew but thanks for our lives." Brain told John all about the phone call from Margaret. John asked, "How did you know?"

"I dreamt it!" She told them and they just looked at her.

"That's the second time, what a wife I've got." They all laughed and life went back to normal.

John got another car and Brain and Sue had no more problems with the gas. Everybody was happy, but Margaret was beginning to dread the phone ringing in case it was the voice and she spent as much time out of her house as possible. She even got a part time job to get out of the house and away from the phone. It worked for almost three months, it was a Saturday morning when the phone rang and John answered it, "It's for you Margaret. You know," he said as he gave her the phone, "the girl on the other end of the line sounds just like you." Margaret went pale, oh no, not again, "Hello Margaret it's been a long time since I rang you last. I've got some very bad news for you. In less then six months we will both be dead. We have a brain tumour."

"Oh no!" then she passed out.

John rushed over to where she lay on the floor and quickly picked her up and laid her on the settee. He picked up the phone, "Hello, hello!" but the phone was dead. John could not bring Margaret round so he called for an ambulance. After doing some tests the doctor told John that they would keep her in for more tests and that they were not sure what was wrong with her. It was about an hour after she came to and when the doctor ask how she felt she said, "Fine, can I go home?" she was told "No" they wanted to find out why she passed out, she never told them of the voice and all the tests came back negative; she had now been in hospital for one week. The doctor came to see her and told her she could go home tomorrow, "We can't find anything wrong with you." When John went to see her that night and was told by the nurse that she was okay he just said "Thank God." And by 11 o'clock the next day Margaret was back in her own home.

Later that day the phone rang and it was the hospital, "Sorry," the nurse said, "The doctor forgot to tell your wife that she is three months pregnant. Congratulations."

"Thank you!" John was over the moon. Margaret did not know, he sat by her side and said, "I bet there's not many men who have to tell their wives this, it's usually the other way round."

She looked at him and said, "Tell me what you're talking about."

"You're going to be a mum! But the nurse said it was a good job you had to go into hospital, if you are to keep the baby you must stop working and rest as much as possible. There are certain foods you must eat and you've got tablets to take. So it was a God's send for sure or you would have lost the baby. The hospital said they looked at your records last time you were in hospital two and a half years ago when you kept getting bad headaches and sore throats, sickness and dizzy spells, were loosing weight and your voice and tired all the time. It was caused by you being pregnant and that's how you lost your baby but not this time, we will go by the book."

They were the happiest couple in the world that day. Margaret had been home almost two weeks when the phone rang. The last two weeks she had felt great and was so happy to be pregnant, it was the best she had felt for over two and a half years. It was great to be alive, in love and having a baby. "Hello Margaret," said Margaret, and a very week voice said, "Yes, how are you?"

"Great. Good," Margaret knew the voice so well.

"I'm ringing to say goodbye – goodbye." But it was very hard to hear what the voice was saying, it was getting more and more distant. What she did pick up was to "Ask Mother about us,"

"Goodbye Margaret, goodbye my sister." and then the phone went dead. She just sat there with tears running down her face. She rang her mother. "Will you come and see me? I need to talk to you, it's very important!"

That night her mum and dad came over to see her and she said to John, "What I am going to tell you, you will be surprised. I would like you to tell my mum about…" then the doorbell rang, "That will be Pat and Bill." Margaret's younger sister and her husband. "Tell me what?" her mother asked.

"My twin sister!"

"How did you find out?"

"She told me."

"What? But she's been dead over 30 years!"

"Yes I know."

"You had a twin and she was born three minutes before you, but before you were born she died. We were going to call you Ann Margaret and your sister Margaret Ann but when we lost her we gave you her name in memory of her. If she had lived you would have the same name but backwards."

"What did she die of?"

"They said a brain tumour."

"She told me that also." then Margaret told them about the phone calls. John just sat there mouth agape, "So she came back from the dead to save lives, but most of all to save your life and our baby's." Part of the nurse's conversation to John was not only would she loose her baby but it also could kill Margaret. But by going to hospital she had saved both of their lives.

Do the dead come back to warn us? You make up your own mind. I've made mine up.

Byy-Way Farm

My name is Morgan Swift, I am a solicitor and I work for Swift and Swift. Swift is my father's firm, he runs the business and I work for him, so it's a family business. We always have plenty of work, and make a good living out of it; we take on almost any case but there have been cases we have turned down, for reasons we won't go into. I lived in a small town called Fellworth, it is near the old main town of Fallington, I am Married to Lucy and have a three year old daughter called Molly. The reason I am telling you this as I would like you to be judge after you have read my story of a case I was on.

The year of my story was 1989. We had a lot of work on our books so we turned this case down, but my father's long time friend asked him to take the case as a favour to him so I got the case. I have done many cases in my time but this case is the strangest one I have ever been asked to do.

As I have said the year was 1989, and on the 28th of May I went to see Jonathan Warrington, a very rich and powerful farmer, who owns a great deal of land around Fellworth. He has three big farms.

The case was about 12 cart horses that Jonathan Warrington had bought; four horses to work on each of his farms. He bought them from a well known horse trader and breeder, a man called Foley Spice, he also was a very rich and powerful man. The case was on the 6th of March 1989. Jonathan Warrington paid cash for the 12 cart horses, but between March 28th and May 2nd four of the horses died – four from the same farm. A vet was called in but he could not say for sure why these four horses died.

He had checked them out and told Jonathan Warrington the 12 horses were in very good health, and he would get a lot of years out of them, so Jonathan bought them. The vet's name was

Alan Miller, a top vet in Fallington. He will tell you that in 1982 he was called out to look at one of the queen's horses, how many times he told that story no one will ever know. Jonathan wanted his money back, saying the 12 horses he bought off Foley Spice were not 100% fit, when he sold them to him, but Foley said he would not pay back one penny. The vet passed them all fit and healthy for any farm work, "Claim your money from him not me. I sold good healthy horses, I will not pay you back a penny. You can take me to court!"

"That I will." Jonathan told him.

My father friend Wally Cane was also a very good friend of Foley Spice who asked him if he knew of a good lawyer, so that is how I got the Warrington and Spice case. Can you follow my story so far? I think so, so on the 28th of May I went to see Foley who was at Warrington Farm for a meeting with Warrington and his lawyer, and wanted me there at the meeting which was to start at eleven o'clock. I got there at 10.30.

Warrington lived in a big mansion on his biggest farm, called Byy-Way Farm. Many years ago the Byy-way family, like Warrington, owned a great deal of land. Warrington kept the name because everyone knew it as Byy-Way Farm. As I walked through the big open oak door into a very large hall, I could hear lots of shouting coming from a room off the hall, so I went into the room and there were many people talking in raised voices, Looking round I saw Warrington his wife and two sons, a solicitor called Henry Bail who I took to be Warrington's lawyer and his sectary,. In the middle of the room I saw Foley Spice, his wife and four sons, also I saw the vet Alan Miller with his lawyer, plus other people I did not know.

No one took any notice of me as I walked into the room, so I walked over to Foley and shook hands, Warrington was now almost shouting, "He was saying 'Shut up, shut up', or 'Get out of here!'"

It was like turning off a light everyone stopped talking, "Good, good!" Warrington shouted looking straight at Foley, "I want my money back or you're a dead man." With that he and his party walked out of the room. The door closed and silence was about them, no one spoke, they just looked at the door.

As Warrington and his party went out, Foley asked me, "Can I come to your office, for now my life might be in danger?"

"Yes, say tomorrow at ten o'clock,"

"Do you not want to talk now?"

"No, tomorrow at ten o'clock." With that he walked away, so I left and went back to my office and told my Father what Warrington had said to Foley Spice. "It doesn't sound good, do you mind if I sit in tomorrow?"

"No I don't mind." Then I got a phone call to go back to the farm, when I asked who I was talking to the phone went dead. I went back to the farm and the door was still open, and again I could hear lots of people shouting, I went back to the room but I could not believe what I saw.

As I walked into the room it was exactly the same as before, everybody was in the same place, and everybody was shouting at each other, but this time everyone was dressed in late 17th century clothing – no one turned to look at me, it was as if I was not there. I walked over to Foley Spice but when I got to him it was as if I was looking in at them as if I was not in the same room; they were in one world and I was looking in at them. From my world I could see them, and hear everything they were saying. Like before, Warrington and his party walked out of the room, and as before, then silence was about them, no one spoke until Foley turned to me. I was looking at myself, I was also dressed in 17th century clothing and as before we shook hands, then Foley said, "Can I come to your office, for now my life is in danger?"

"Yes"

"Say tomorrow at ten o'clock." Then the next thing I knew I was outside the mansion getting into my car. My mind was blank, to me it was as if this was my first call at the mansion.

It was not until I was at my office, when my father came in and said, "How did you get on? Who was it who rang you?" then it all came back to me. I told my father about my first visit to the mansion, he just looked at me, then said, "If you were not my son I would think you had lost it completely. You know many years ago my grandfather told me of a murder at the farm that you were at. In those days the farm was called Byy-Way Farm,"

"It still is,"

"But they called it Way Back Byy-Way Farm, it did not click 'til you told me your story," calling out, my father said to our secretary, "I want you to find out everything you can about Byy-Way Farm. I want you to go way back as far as you can. Do it as quickly as you can, it is very important. As soon as you have the information bring it to me please."

With that our secretary left the office, "How many murders were there?"

"I think there were two,"

"Who were they?"

"I don't know, but if I no Jean," Jean was his secretary, "She will find out, we just have to wait." So most of the afternoon I just got on with my work, but before I did I made a recording on tape, telling everything of my two visits to the farm. My father took the tape into his office to listen to them. Later he said, "I've listen to it twice, I think it's a call for help, I bet one of the people murdered in the past has something to do with horses, so does the second person murdered."

"What makes you say that?"

"I read a lot of books on the dead asking the living to help them move on as they are trapped in a world they can't escape from."

The world of the dead, "But why come to us?"

"That I don't know, but I'm sure Jean will give us the information we are looking for."

Jean rang "I am sure I've got it all."

"Good girl."

"Where are you?"

"Just leaving the library now, see you in 20 minutes." What a story she was to tell us both, so she recorded the information she had:

"The life and death of Thomas Henry, Byy-Way Farm.
And life and death of Father and Son.
Sidon Michal – Co land Michal.

"Thomas Henry Byy-Way bought a great deal of land in and around Fellworth between 1689 and 1690, where he built a very big mansion and farm. At the time it was rumoured that Thomas Henry Byy-Way was once a pirate, and made a very big fortune on gold and silver Coins, diamonds, rubies, peals, he had a big chest full to the brim with treasures, worth in those days thousands upon thousands pounds. Today's value would be millions, in the 16th to 17th century, Fellworth was called Fiel-woth. Thomas Henry Byy-Way had six big coloured men as his body guards, there were rumours that other pirates were looking for him, but that was all that was known about him. Wherever Thomas Henry Byy-Way went so did these six men. They guarded him 24 hours a day, right up until he died. After his death the six men left the mansion and were never seen again.

"In 1695 Thomas Henry Byy-Way married Lord Declare's daughter, Evener. It was said that Lord Declare was in a lot of debt, owing a large amount of money to a lot of people who were pressing him hard for their money. So Thomas Henry Byy-Way gave Lord Declare a great deal of money to marry his daughter Evener to pay off all his debt and have enough money to live on. Thomas Henry and Evener had a good, long and happy life together, having four boys and four girls. In 1750 Evener died of an unknown flu-like virus.

In 1700 Thomas Henry started his second farm, and five years later in 1705 the third farm. All the three Farms were called Byy-

Way Farms. In 1755 Thomas Henry died of old age, they say he was between 85 to 90 years old. On one of his farms he bred and showed cart horses and they won many trophies over the years. They won prizes all over the country. He bred these horses for many years, then in 1730 he sold all his horses, no one knows why, only keeping about 10 to 15 of these horses, then on two of his farms he started to breed sheep.

"His four daughters all got married, two moved to France, one moved to Spain, and the fourth daughter moved to Ireland. As for his four sons, one went to London and was shot dead playing cards, one went to Germany and married a German girl, opened his own farm and stayed there for the rest of his life, and the other two sons stayed and ran the three farms between them.

In 1767 one of his sons died; he was killed by a runaway bull. The first son born was named after his father Thomas Henry Byy-Way Junior, in 1772 Thomas Henry Junior bought 12 cart horses for his farms, he went to an old friend of his father, a man called Sidon who also breeds cart horses. His father's friend Sidon also had a lot of land and was very rich, Thomas Henry Junior got his 12 cart horses in December 1772 but a month later four of the horses died, no one knew why or ever found out. There was a big row between Thomas Henry Junior and the man called Sidon.

Thomas Henry Junior asked Sidon for his money back, but Sidon would not give him the money back for the four dead horses. Thomas Henry Junior said, "If you don't give me back my money you are a dead man," but Sidon would not give back the money. In January of 1773 Sidon was found dead, with a pitchfork in his back, but it could not be proven that Thomas Byy-Way killed him or had had Sidon killed, so Thomas Henry Junior never went to court or prison.

"In February of 1773 Sidon's dodgy solicitor was found drowned in a local river, again there was no case against Thomas Henry

Junior. There were a lot of people who hated Sidon and his dodgy solicitor, who was called Girgan Hadfe. In 1785 Thomas Henry Junior sold all his land, animals and mansion to Samuel Warrington. There were rumours that Girgan Hadfe went to Thomas Henry Junior and told him in anger that he knew he had Sidon killed, and he could prove it unless he gave him £1,000, and as I told you, in February 1773 Girgan Hadfe was found drowned in a local river.

"All was well until 1786 when Samuel Warrington bought 10 cart horses. Thomas Henry Byy-Way Junior's family owned all the land for almost 100 years, but his family moved away – where? No one knows. The man who took Sidon's land, farms and horses was a young man from Bedfordshire called Co land, he sold 10 horses to Samuel Warrington – now this is where history repeats itself, in March 1786 he got his 10 horses, but at the end of May four of the horses were dead, and again no one knew why, or ever found out, and like Thomas Henry Byy-Way wanted his money back for the four dead hoses, but Co land said "No, no money back," and again the two men had a big row where Samuel Warrington said "My money back or you're a dead man!" In July Co land was found dead shot in the head, again no one could prove Warrington killed Co land or had had him killed, there was no court case to answer too, but again rumours that a lot of money changed hands.

"In September Co land's solicitor was found hanging from Co land's barn. "

Jean then said "See what I mean about history repeating itself, here's a little twist to the story,"

"Sidon's past before he moved to Fellworth was a highwayman, he made lots of money and moved to Fellworth were no one knew him or of him, his Christian name became his surname his real name was Sidon Michel, Co land who took over his land and farms real name is Co land Michel, Sidon Michel was Co land's father, both bad men and both died over horses, after the horses had been sold. As I said history repeating itself, not only father and son but both of their solicitors. Well that's it and as you know the land, mansion and farms still belong to the Warrington family to this day."

I looked at my father, "Well there's one for the books,"

"How right you are,"

"Now what do I do?"

"We will have to think what to do."

"Shall we call in the church?" We both thanked Jean for what she had done, and she said, "I was happy to help,"

"We will tell you everything once we close this case," and at the moment I have not got a clue. "Right point one," my father said "Father and son killed over horses, point two you went to the farm twice, first time in 1989 and spoke to Foley Spice the man who sold Warrington the horses who died, point three there was an unknown phone call to go back to the farm, point four, you went back and saw the same people but it was as if you were looking into their world, but at a moment in time; you went into their world, spoke to Foley Spice – the same conversation as before, it was like watching a repeat on T.V., point five, but this time you were dressed in 17th century clothing, how am I doing?

"O.K."

"Good, point six, we now know this is history repeating itself through the years of 1773-1787 and now 1989 – no not 1989, no deaths yet,"

"Sorry you're right, but the first two are the same as number three;"

"Yes you're right,"

"But how do we stop number 3?"

"Where do we start? I would say go and see Warrington and let him read Jean's report."

"That's one way, but Foley Spice also must read Jean's report, so he will know what he is up against,"

"You're right." my father said, "I think this case need both of us on it," I was happy to hear him say that.

"O.K., yes, two is better than one."

"Right let's wait until tomorrow, Foley will be here at ten o'clock, right now it's six o'clock: time to go home. If you do think of anything put it down on paper."

With that the three of us went home, I could not sleep that night thinking of the case we had taken on.

We sat in my office the next day waiting for Foley to come and at ten o'clock he walked into my office. My father said to Foley, "Read Jean's report, then we will tell you what's going on."

After reading the report he asked. "Is this for real?"

"Yes, Jean got all this information from the library."

"What about the dress, and you in one world and me in another?"

"I know it's very hard to believe."

"Yes I know, but it's the truth."

"Have you any idea what killed the horses?"

"Well I've got three ideas of what may have killed them; some kind of poison given to them by Sidon before he sold them, or he paid a farm hand to kill them, or – a long shot –there was something on the farm that killed them,"

"Such as?"

"I don't know, but it has happened three times. That's what makes me think there's something on the land."

"What will we do now? We can't prove anything with Sidon or Co land, they are dead, but what if I go to Warrington and asked him to have his land checked out?"

"Do you think he will let you?"

"The only way I will know is to ask him, but before I do I will ask Jean to get maps of Warrington's farm land."

"Why?"

"Well let's say once we know the lay out of his land we can asked him to show us where the horses died. Then we can go from there."

"Where to?"

"I don't know, but it's a start."

"If you have a better idea tell us."

"No, no."

"What have we got to lose?"

"In fact I think it's not a bad idea,"

"Good, Jean has a list of the births and deaths of Thomas Byy-Way and the Warrington Family. Have a look at it, you can keep it, We have copyies."

This is Jean's report

Thomas Henry Byy-Way sold his land to Samuel Warrington in 1785.

Samuel Warrington died in 1830, left the farm to his son Denial Warrington.

Denial Warrington died in 1850, left farm to his son Richmond Warrington.

Richmond Warrington died in 1900, left farm to his son Roy Don Warrington

Roy Don Warrington died in 1942, left farm to his son Jonathan Warrington.

Jonathan Warrington still alive, running Byy-Way Farm. 1989.

"Tell you what, you know your business. I'm very happy you took my case on, there's a lot to do yet but see what comes of our visit to Byy-Way Farm. One thing I don't want you to do is talk about your case to anyone, the more people don't know about the case the better; not even your wife. When she asks just tell her when we know something we will let her know."

"O.K, thank you." So for the next hour we asked Foley lots of questions. After he had left my father said, "He is an honest man, he never harmed those horses, I bet my life on it."

The only thing we have to do is prove it. "How long will it take Jean to get the plans of Byy-Way Farm?"

"If I know Jean, not long. I've made all the calls to the town hall."

"I know a few people."

"Good, Jean rang – I'll have copies of the plans by late afternoon, do you want me to bring them to the office?"

"Yes, as soon as you can, get a cab back."

"O.K., When will you ring Warrington?"

"As soon as we have the plans of his farm, I want to go there knowing where everything is, like cow sheds, chicken sheds, pig pen, and horses stables, and where the farm houses were on his land and so on. We must find out how much Foley sold his horses for, how old they were, and does he have a history of breeding horses, and if so did he breed the horses he sold to Warrington."

Later Foley rang and asked if he could put back tomorrow's meeting from ten o'clock to twelve o'clock. "Yes that will be fine," I then told him what information I wanted from him.

"I'll bring it all in with me tomorrow." I spent the rest of the day doing paperwork from other cases, Jean got back to the office at six o'clock with all the papers we wanted, it was late so we decided to leave everything until tomorrow.

At nine o'clock sharp we were ready to go. Jean came into the office with a folder "Right I've got a lot to tell you. First I rang Zola Zanfield and asked her if she can pop round and see me last night and she did. Zola Zanfield is a 60 year old woman, married with two children, Steven and Patsy, what Zola doesn't know about ghosts, sprits, the dark world, death, you could put on a penny. first I showed her the map of Byy-Way Farm. There are two ways into Byy-Way Farm; from the north end of town follow main road, left at Kings Pub or the south end of the main road, turn right at the Old Mill restaurant then onto a country lane called Avian Way Lane. It's wide enough for two cars to pass though it twists and bends for nearly two miles, it brings you right in front of the mansion. Next I've got 10 drawings and photos of Warrington and his sons, who over the years ran Byy-Way Farms, and drawings of the old mansion in the 17th century and photos of it today, I also have drawings of what Sidon and Co land might have looked like, and the same for this two solicitors, finally and drawings of what Thomas Henry Byy-Way might have looked like, and photos of Foley Spice.

"It's now gone 12 o'clock Foley Spice had not turned up, so while we are waiting for him I'll tell you what Zola Zanfield told me. I told her about Byy-Way, Warrington and Foley Spice and the dead horses, first she closed her eyes and ran her hand all over the map, then she stopped and put a red cross on the map and were she put the red cross was a field. She said no living man killed these horses, the field is evil and has death in it, 'You must check, this but be careful my friend, be very careful.' Looking at the photos and drawings she touched each one, 'You must not go today,' then she said to tell Mr Swift his first visit to the farm was in this world, but the second visit, as soon as he went back into the mansion he went back to a meeting held in the 17th century, that's why all their clothing was of the 17th century. When he walked out of the mansion he was back in his own time, the phone call that Mr Swift got was from another world, I do not know at this moment the full reason but we do know you were to go back to the mansion for the second time.

"She also said to look at the Warrington Family: all the fathers and sons are like peas in a pod. Zola read the transcript of your tape that I typed up, and said 'Yes, it's the past you must go to.'"

It was gone twelve o'clock when the phone rang, it was Foley's wife saying that he had been in a car accident but was on his way to the office, "He's O.K. but the car is a write-off, the police say they don't know how he walked away with not a scratch, he will be with you about two o'clock, is that O.K.?"

"Yes, that's fine."

"He said to tell you he has all the paperwork you wanted with him."

I hung up the phone and then Jean continued "Zola also said go back onto Fellworth land to find your answer, now I must go."

and with that she left, calling over her shoulder, "I rang Patrick O Conner, a historian and arranged a meeting with him at 4 o'clock this afternoon." We just looked at Jean,. My father said, "What would we do without her?" Laughing, Jean said "Answering the phone, typing, going to the library, making the tea, sorting out the mail, paying the bills, making the appointments…"

"O.K., O.K., you win!" Just then, Foley and his wife walked in, so we repeated to them what Jean had told us. We checked out the bill of sale and the health certificate for the horses and they were all legal. "Give us a few days, we will know more by then."

A little while later Foley and his wife left, "I think we will put off ringing Mr Warrington until we see what Jean and Mr O Conner come up with."

When Jean came in to the office next morning, this is what she had typed, from her meeting with Mr O Conner:

The Battle Cogan 1127

In the 11th century Wellworth was called Cogan, after King Cogan; a big powerful evil king he stood 7ft tall, and weighed around 30 stone. He had thick long red hair and a beard. If his people did not do what he told them to do he tortured them and put them to death. He was the most feared king in middle England, He became king in 1097, it is said he killed his father over land in 1122, and his younger brother Titian said to him 'Stop the torture and the killing.' but he laughed at Titian and said, "I am king, I'll do what I want. If you don't like it leave my land or I will kill you too." So Titian left and many followed him.

He went to a far away land, and built and trained a great army. In 1127 he returned to Cogan to do battle. Halfway through the battle King Cogan knew he was going to lose, so he sent a message to Titian saying "Let us do combat, if you win you become king, if I win you die." So on the 11th of June 1127 King Cogan and Titian stood facing each other. Cogan called out, "You little fool, death stands waiting!" but as Cogan rushed at Titian with his big sword above his head Titian struck his sword into Cogan's stomach. The great evil man fell dying to the ground.

He cried out, "On this day you shall never win, for I curse this ground were I lay and die, no grass, tree, or bush shall live, no bird, animal, or man shall ever survive this curse for 1000 years!" then King Cogan died. Where his brother fell Titian had him buried and he put up a fence and he had a great stone laid on top of his brother's grave, "So all shall know were my brother lays." Titian was a good king, there was no more torture or killings. He was king for 40 years but never once went back to the Field of Death, as he called it.

We all looked at Jean, "Now we've got to check the cross on the map, ask Warrington if he knows the story about Cogan and Titian and the curse, and if he ever put his horses in that field." So Jean rang Jonathan Warrington and asked him if he put the horses in that field and he said yes, so a day later with my father, the maps, and all our findings, we went to Byy-Way Mansion.

As soon as we got there and met Jonathan Warrington we both liked him. He was 5ft tall and built like a beer barrel with little legs and short arms, and a contagious smile. A man of truth, for over two hours we talked and he read all our notes and looked at the drawings and photos and the maps of Byy-Way Farm, he looked at the red cross and said, "O my God, my horses were put in that field for three days a week, later they were all dead!"

"Do you think a member of your family put your horses in that field and they all died?"

Jonathan Warrington just sat looking at that field with the red cross, he said, "I've done Foley Spice a great injustice, I must call him right away."

"It would be better if you asked him to call on you, for we think you could be very good friends, and who knows you might even buy more horses from him."

"Well, we can't prove whether his sons did put the horses in that field, the Field of Death, Warrington did have people in to look at the field and they reported that they do not know why nothing will grow, or why the earth is like dust and dry so nothing can be grown in it, they said "What causes this we do not know, but while we were in the field we felt ill, once out of the field we all felt O.K. again."

Warrington said because it was a barren field he never, nor could he remember his father ever using it.

So like every strange story there is a twist. Four evil men died for something they did not do, did others kill them hoping that Byy-Way and Warrington would get the blame? As you know, no one was ever charged, but that's not the end of my story. My father and I asked Jean, if she would like to become a partner, in our company we were very pleased when she said yes, and as her daughter was looking for work she also came to work for us – she was a lawyer. We don't know why but since the Warrington and Foley Spice case we are snowed under with work.

Well that is my story, I hope you enjoyed reading it. Just a quick note, in 1772-1786-1989 it strange because only four of the horses died on each of these dates. Why four?

Crayford Hall

Crayford Hall was built in 1710 for the children of Crayford village and villagers nearby. It was built to hold 20 children but on many occasions, it had anything from 30 to 40 children. It was built for the children who had nowhere to sleep, no home, no mother or father, or friends to take them in. It was a poor house. It was a cold, hard place to live, for the children worked long hours, were beaten and were not allowed to talk until the day was over and all the work was done. They worked seven days a week and everyday children were brought back after running away, to more beatings, or put in the hole. The hole was a cell in the basement, it was dark, cold and you only had straw to sleep on and one old blanket. You could be put in the hole for anything and be down there for up to a month. Many poor children died down there, no one knew and no one would've cared, for they would say he or she ran away and they could not find them, or they had gone to live with rich people. Many children disappeared over the 10 years it was open. It was built by Lord Crayford who lived at Crayford Manor just outside Crayford Village. He once said, "I don't want my friends from London to see dirty, scruffy little kids running around the village begging."

So he built Crayford Hall for little, lost, lonely, hungry children of his village and the nearby villages, and all his friends said, "What a good man Lord Crayford is." It finally closed down in 1720, when old Lord Crayford died. For over 110 years lots of stories were told about Crayford Hall, homes for the poor, lost children and that's how Lord Crayford used to talk about the hall. To the villages it was called the Hell House of Crayford. The new Lord Crayford sold it to a horse dealer who in less than a year was found hanging from a beam. He told a friend late at night he could hear children crying and calling for their mothers, and had started to drink heavily, then one day he never turned up at the horse trade market. His friend went to Crayford Hall and found him hanging.

The hall stayed empty until 1724, when it was again bought by the third Lord Crayford, who made it into a tavern as it was on the old London road (Crayford is just over 20 miles from Bristol, and from Crayford to London is about 150 miles). The road at that time was the main Bristol to London road. It was used by the Romans many years before. The road was used almost by everyone, coaches, horse carts carrying hay, farm vegetables, wood, and sheep. Highwaymen made a living off the road. Lord Crayford opened it as a tavern, knowing it would make him a lot of money, which it did. He called the Tavern 'The Gold Mine', for he did not want people to know what it used to be or its past.

He made sure all his friends knew of the tavern, and served only the best food and wine, and hired the best looking girls he could find to work in the tavern. It was the best tavern for many miles around and every night it was packed with all kinds of people. He went only once to the tavern to put his plans to work. He had the week's takings taken to his manor every eighth day; it did not take long for the highwaymen to find this out. He knew this so he got them to work for him, he would buy all the booty then say to people who had been robbed, "I may be able to get your possessions back, but it may cost you!" Sooner than let on that they have been robbed to their friends, they paid, and Lord Crayford always made good money and they thought he was their friend and saviour, but it was whispered over a glass of ale that he was in line with the highwaymen, but no one dared say it because Lord Crayford was a very rich and powerful man, who was well-liked and well-known in London and leant large amounts of money to lords, ladies and even royalty. By using his money he got power and that got him into the Royal Court. Whatever was going on he was always in the middle, offering his help and his money. He was a very cleaver man, so by getting friends by using his money no one would say a word against him, for if they did they knew they would be out of the circle, and no one wanted that.

It was in 1742, almost 15 years had gone by and Lord Crayford was now one of the most powerful men in London, and was known all over England. The tavern could tell many stories, for it was also known far and wide. Many deals were made at the tavern over a hot meal and a jug of ale. One night two men were playing cards, one a highwayman, the other a sheep trader, the highwayman lost a lot of money, for he could just not win, so he started to cheat and got all his money back plus most of the sheep trader's money, but in one game the sheep trader caught him cheating and a fight started. The highwayman was no match for the sheep trader, so he pulled out is pistol and short dead the trader. The next night the trader's brother went to the tavern looking for the highwayman, the highwayman saw him at the tavern door looking for him, so as the brother turned to close the tavern door, the highwayman shot the brother dead, he shot him in the back!

When Lord Crayford heard, he sent his men to arrest the highwayman, whose name was Ben Gally, the sheep trader's name was Cart May. But as Lord's Crayford's got to the tavern the highwayman opened up with his pistols, killing one man, but as he tried to run he was shot dead. Another highwayman hanged himself over one of the tavern girls in an upstairs room; Lord Crayford by now had as many enemies as friends.

It was in April 1742 that while out riding a man ran up to him and shot him dead. They never found out who killed him or why, but a lot of people knew and were very happy over his death. The fourth Lord Crayford was a fool of a man and lost all of his money at cards and horses, and had to sell the tavern to cover his debts. The tavern lay empty for 12 years.

In 1756 a carpenter bought the tavern and for the next 40 years it stayed as a store workshop, repairing coaches, fences, carts, windows, woodwork and many other things. In that 40 years one man working at the back of the old tavern cut his throat, another shot himself, one went insane crying out "Save the children, save the children!" It finally closed in 1818 and was turned into a barn. But it was not often used. It again stayed as a barn until 1830. By 1835, five years later it remained empty, it was beginning to look in a terrible state, for time and weather had taken its toll on the old building.

In 1836, a farmer wanted to convert it into a cottage, and spent a lot of time making it good enough to live in again, but fate was there again; the farmer was found dead in the cellar. It was now 1840, the old London road was not being used very much. The countryside was changing fast. A retired army officer and his wife bought it and moved in. But within five years his wife went mad, and had to be put in a hospital where she killed herself. The army officer lived alone in the cottage, but he also went mad. The villages used to say "He was talking to the children again, he would say 'I know every child who lived here, they told me all about Crayford Hall, They want me to go with them'." He was found hanged.

In 1858 again it laid empty. By now no one wanted to buy the cottage or go near it. It lay empty until 1866 when the church bought it very cheap. They wanted it as a school house, and again had it repaired and made a garden in front of the school, planted trees, bushes and flowers and made the place look very nice. It opened as a day school in September 1868. All was well until 1870, then things started to go wrong. One boy whose father was well-off said "Someone pushed me down the stairs!" but no one was there, I know as everyone was in the schoolroom, Another boy said he was locked in the bedroom, "I heard the lock turn," but there was no key to lock the door, it went missing years ago. A fire started in the kitchen, but no fire was on, and no one was in the kitchen.

A farmer's dog would not go to near the school. A horseman was riding past the school, when suddenly the horse threw it's rider off, killing him. The horse was found dead the next day. Another farmer, out with his dog, saw a little girl of about seven years old sitting on the grass crying, "I called out to her, she looked up, my dog started barking, I turned around to tell him to stop. When I looked back the little girl had gone." The first school teacher, a middle-aged lady died within a week.

A doctor took over, waiting for a new teacher to arrive. He said, "I was reading my paper, next I looked up a small boy was by my side. He said, "Sir can I have some food for my sister?"

"I said "Yes come with me. Where is your sister?" I got up, and he was gone, I looked around but never found him." The doctor left the school, A few days later they found him dead in bed.

Nothing happened for the next five years, but in those five years children became ill and some would not go to school. Over 20 children had accidents. In that five years the school had a new teacher almost every six months, at the end of 1876 the church closed the school down. It was put up for sale, but no one wanted to buy it. Finally in 1880, having been empty for almost four years, a sailor bought it, "Ghosts don't bother me. I love kids; you'll see, I'll have them swabbing the decks in no time." And true to is word he lived there for the next 20 years. In one letter to his sister he wrote:

I've got all the children to learn my sea songs. They can dance, I play the piano accordion, they laugh and sing and we have lots of fun playing games, hide and seek, but I cannot touch them and they cannot touch me. We can see each other, talk to each other, but if there's a knock at the door they run and then they are gone it may be days until I see them again, I know all their names, they call me Captain Sam.

One of his songs he used to sing to the children went something like this;-

Captain Sam Captain Sam went to sea in an old tin can,
The sea is blue, the sea is deep,
That's where all the big fishes go to sleep.

He flies his flag of fish and whale,
And when he's in port tells many a tale,
Does Captain Sam Captain Sam.

He bobs up and down in his old tin can,
And all the sailors cry out,
'Look there's Captain Sam!'

A sailor's life is ever so grand,
But sometime they wish,
They were on dry land,
Says Captain Sam.

But now he's home and on dry land,
He plays with the children, from a time gone by,
And makes them laugh instead of cry,
Captain Sam Captain Sam.

They would jump and laugh and clap their hands,
Shout and sing 'Play it again Captain Sam,
Sing it again Captain Sam,'
Then they would start again and sing,
Captain Sam Captain Sam he bobs up and down in his old tin
can……

Another little song:

I'll teach you to sing, I'll teach you to dance,
We won't do it once we'll do it twice,
We'll dance round the deck, we'll dance round the cook,
We'll dance round the captain while he's reading his book,
We'll jump up and down and all spin round,
Then the last man to fall and sit on the deck,
Will get a bucket of water tipped down his neck.

Silly little songs but the children loved them.
Another little song:

The sail got a hole in it,
What shall we do?
I've got a needle,
I've got the twine,
We can sow it up,
In half the time.

I've got no shoes,
I've got no vest,
But I've got a captain,
Who is the best,
I've got no bed,
I've got no chair,
But I've got the best captain,
So I don't care.

I've never had butter,
I've never had ham,
But I've got the best,
I've got Captain Sam,
Captain Sam Captain Sam.

36

It was Captain Sam in every verse they would sing 'Captain Sam he was the best.' There was no rest only Captain Sam, Captain Sam Captain Sam over and over again, the children would sing, sing and sing.

In 1900 Captain Sam died.

In 1901 the house was bought by John Barnes and his partner Will Riley. They bought sheep and cows from the farmer, took them to London and sold them. They made a good living, as there were always people in London wanting to buy livestock. They used the cottage as an office, and sometimes lived their.

John Barns was married with one child; a little girl called Dorothy. Will Riley was single. They got on well as they both knew a lot about buying and selling sheep, cows, goats, horses, even chickens and rabbits now and then, but sheep were their main business. They had been partners for nearly three years, and had made a great deal of money between them in that short time. But the start of the fourth year things did not go as they had hoped, the sheep market started to fall off, cows and goats almost came to a standstill; horses were taken over by rail and motors, so they were wanted fewer, and fewer.

In London you still had horse and carts; Hanson Cab used horses but most other transport was by motorbuses that took people all over London. So they decided to split the money and each go their own way. The money was around £35,000, not bad for nearly four years together in the very late 18th century, but Will Riley disappeared – there one day, gone the next with all the money. They did not keep the money in the bank, but in a safe in the cottage; John Barnes called the police, but they could not find Will or the money. The police were not happy with John's story but had no proof of anything to go on so they shut the file on Will Riley. John had work done on the cottage and lived there with his wife and little girl. Then his wife started to act funny and he had her put in a mental home, where in 1920 she died. She used to say "Nurse can I have more food, the children are hungry?" They would just look at her and say "Poor things," and carry on with their duties.

In 1921 John Barnes closed up the cottage, and sent his daughter to France while he went to live in London. Dorothy by now was 22 years old, and while in France she met and fell in love with a school teacher, called Jean Guy St Clare, who liked to be called Guy. In 1924 they got married, but that same year her father died, he ran out in front of a car and was killed outright, so Dorothy and Guy returned to England and had her father's will read. In the will it said "To my only daughter Dorothy Barnes", for he did not know of her marriage as they did not see or hear from him after Dorothy went to France, "I leave Pine Cottage and £30,000, God bless you, your father, John Barnes." and that was what the will said. So Dorothy and Guy moved into pine cottage. It was only by chance that John met an old friend in London who told him about his wife and daughter living in France. When John was killed, his friend went through his clothing and found the address of Dorothy in France.

Martin and Jane Powers both worked in the local hospital, Martin was a male nurse and Jane a matron. They were both in their 40s, the only child they had died during a very difficult birth, and as a result Jane could not have anymore children. Not being able to have children made them very close, for they lived for one another. They both did day work at the hospital so they went to the hospital together and came home at night together; they never went anywhere unless they went together. One evening after they had just got home, the phone rang, it was Barry and Brown, Town Solicitors. "Is that Mr Power, Martin Power?"

"Yes, speaking."

"Is it possible I could pop round to night to see you and your wife?"

"Could you tell me why?"

"Don't worry Mr Power, nothing is wrong."

"Okay then say eight o'clock."

"Great see you at eight.". At eight o'clock sharp the door bell rang, "Hello, I'm Peter Berry."

"Come in,"

"Thank you." After they had chatted for a while, Peter Berry opened his briefcase, "I would like to ask you both some questions, do you mind?"

"No ask away, if we can help we will!"

"Do you know a Mrs Dorothy St Clare?"

"Yes,"

"I believe you both got to know Mrs St Clare in hospital where she was a patient,"

"Yes,"

"You both got to know her well?"

"Yes,"

"You both became good friends with Mrs St Clare?"

"Yes,"

"You both used to visit her on your time off duty?"

"Yes,"

"And your days off?"

"Yes,"

"I have it in my report that Mrs St Clare died in her sleep."

"Yes, yes that's right."

"I also have that she was 81 years old."

"We think so, but do not know for sure, she told us she was 81, but you know old people, don't like to give there real age. But as far as we know yes. She was eighty-one years old. Does it matter?"

"Yes and no. Did you know that she was a widow?"

"Yes,"

"She had no children as far as you two know?"

"As far as she told us she did not have any children."

"Do you know if she had any relations alive, that we would not know of?"

"As far as we know she had no one, if she did she never told us of them."

"Well as far as we could find out she does not have any." Jane asked "Mr Berry what's all this about?"

"I'm just about to come to that. I've got some very good news for you both.

"Mrs St Clare left a will and in the will, Mrs St Clare has left her cottage and £70,000 to Martin and Jane Power. All you two have to do is prove you are Martin and Jane Power, sign some forms and the cottage and money are yours. There is also a letter to you, we do not know what is in the letter, as it is addressed to you both. Can you come to my office Thursday say ten o'clock? I've checked, it's both your days off. The reason I want you both at my office is so we have a witness to say the letter was not opened, and to give you Mrs St Clare's will. Is that okay?"

"Yes."

"Good see you both Thursday at 10 in my office. I have to go as I have to see someone else before I can go home!" With that he was up and gone. For the rest of that evening that's all the Powers talked about. The will, the cottage and of course the £70,000, and what was in the letter at Berry and Brown the solicitors?

By eleven o'clock that Tursday they were on their way home. They read the letter again, this is what was in Mrs Dorothy St Clare's letter:

Mrs Dorothy St Clare

To my dear friends Martin and Jane Powers, when you both receive my last letter I will have left this world and moved on to the next. In this world I have no family of my own that I know of. I was not a very good friend-maker, as I always liked to keep myself to myself. When I lost my husband I lost interest in the human race even though I am one of them. In my own way I enjoyed my way of living here on Earth, but now it's coming to an end. I have no regrets about leaving but strange as it may seem I feel very happy to leave knowing I am leaving something to two wonderful people, who I have become very fond of, and those two people are of course, you Martin and Jane. Thank you both for being so kind to me and for the many times you came to see me in hospital, I think I laughed more times in hospital with you two than in all my lifetime put together. It is sad when you can count your true friends on one hand, but I only need two fingers to count two true friends. If all has gone to plan my solicitor would have seen you both, Berry and Brown, and will be reading my letter to you both.

Please Martin and Jane except my gift to you for I will be looking down on you both, and once I hear you both say yes I can rest in peace in my new world. Thank you both from my old, but happy heart. Please say yes!

Your friend
'til we meet again
Mrs Dorothy St Clare
21st May 1988.

Pine Cottage was the only cottage in Wood Moor Lane, all the rest were bungalows and houses. The cottage was a very old building, but it had been looked after very well. There was a very large back garden, a nice size front garden, again both looked after. There were four bedrooms upstairs and a box room, downstairs a large front room, and a spacious kitchen at the back. The front room had a large picture window, the downstairs toilet was between the front room and the kitchen. In the toilet there was a bath, toilet, shower and sink, and you still had room. All this work on the cottage had only been done in the last six years. It also had a very large cellar with four small rooms, very small rooms. You could go down to the cellar from inside the cottage or from a pull-up door just outside the kitchen door. Also from the front room was a very large fireplace. The ceiling had large wooden beams going across the ceiling and at one time it looked like hooks had hung from the ceiling by the fireplace. It was said that many years ago it was a highwayman's tavern or a hide up from the law. It is also said the cottage had been many things over the years.

Dorothy St Clare's husband had died at the cottage, they had only been living there six months, when one day her husband had been hit by something on the head while working in the back garden. Dorothy found him lying in a pool of blood, all she could get from him was "I heard a child call, I looked up but no one was there, then I felt a terrible pain in my head", but nothing could be found to have cut his head open, so it was put down as a violent brainstorm. He died the next day. Dorothy carried on living at the cottage right up until she went into hospital. Martin and Jane went to look at the cottage, which was on the other side of town, that weekend. "When can we move in?" Jane asked Martin.

"As soon as we can." he said,

"But what shall we do with our house?"

"I think for a while we will keep it!" They both agreed. Six weeks later the Powers moved into the cottage. It took almost a week to get the cottage how they wanted it, but at last it was all done.

It was about six weeks later that Jane was in the kitchen and Martin was in the front room reading the paper, when something made him look up and there, only a few feet away from him, looking at him was a little girl. She looked for about half a minute then turned and ran off, then completely disappeared. "Jane quickly, come here!" When Jane came in he told her what had happen; she just looked at him, "I wasn't going to say anything but last week I saw the same little girl in the kitchen, who is she?" Jane asked. But they could find no answer.

A few days later she stood in front of Martin, but this time she did not run off; Martin didn't know what to do. He just said, "Hello, what's your name?" The little girl just looked at him. Martin said, "My name is Martin." again nothing from the little girl. Martin called Jane, Jane answered back "I'm at the door, I can see the little girl." the little girl looked at Jane, Jane said "Hello I'm Jane, what's your name?" But the little girl turned and ran off again, completely disappearing.

Again they could not come up with answers. It was three days later, Martin this time was in the kitchen, again something made him look round, and again the little girl was there, but this time she had with her a little boy holding her hand. Martin guessed the little girl to be about six years old, and the little boy about four years old. "Hello," said Martin, "You brought your little friend with you, hello I'm Martin," and again, after about a minute, this time they both turned and were gone. When Jane came in from the garden he told her. "Do you think they lived here years ago?" asked Jane.

"No idea" said Martin. The next day the little girl and boy suddenly were there, standing in front of Martin, but behind them were about 12 other children, all looking at Martin, but not saying a word. But this time Jane was in the room, she was the first to speak, "Hello, I see you brought your friends with you. Hello I'm Jane and this is Martin,"

"Hello," Martin said "Won't you tell us your names?" and again they turned round and were gone.

The Powers did not see the children for almost a week, when suddenly they were there, but this time there were about 20 children and again just standing there looking at Jane and Martin. Martin said "Hello children," then suddenly the little girl said, "My name is Mary and this is my little brother Ben. Will you play with us?"

"We would love too," said Jane. "What shall we play, hide and seek?" All the children started laughing, and jumping up and down Mary said, "We'll hide and you come find us". Jane and Martin could see the children and could hear them speak, but could not touch them. It was the same for the children, they could see and hear but could not touch Jane and Martin. They were real ghosts, it was a strange game of hide and seek when you can't touch the children, but it was fun playing with them.

They all gave there names and ages, but would not answer any other questions. They would just stand looking at Jane and Martin then run off. At first it was very hard trying to get to know the children, but very slowly they started to relax and would sing the Sailor Sam song to them. Jane loved to listen to them. It was now nearly a month since little Mary first stood in front of Martin. "This is wrong." Jane said one night while they were having a meal out. "We are playing with the living dead."

"But what can we do?" Martin asked.

"We will call in our local vicar, he will know what to do." They both agreed. So they rang the vicar and asked him to pop round, but didn't tell him about the children. He said "I'll be round Sunday afternoon."

"Good" said Jane "That gives us five days to work out how we are going to tell him about the children. The children will not show themselves to him so it's going to be hard to tell him," On Saturday morning a letter came for them addressed to Mr & Mrs Powers. Jane opened it and called out to Martin "It's from Mrs St Clare."

"Read it out Jane." So Jane read the letter, this is what was written:

"To My Dearest Friends,

First I owe you both an apology for not telling you both everything about the cottage. Please dear friends do not think badly of me, for if I have told you, you might have turned my gift down. I would like to start from when the cottage was first built in the 17th century…"

The letter went on right up to just before she died, mostly about the children, for she had checked the history of the cottage form the library and old cuttings found in an old box in the cellar and what she had learnt from different people in the town, also from the papers. She went on to say that it was after her husband died that she first saw the children and of course she knew all about them. She herself had tried to get the children exorcised, but whatever she tried failed, "…and being that you two people's lives are dedicated to looking after the sick and old, I thought you would be the right people to help release those poor, poor little children. Please dear friends just for me. You are the only people, if it can be done, do it. I did not leave my cottage to you both just to help the children I gave you my home because I really do think highly of you both. And even without the children, my home was yours. Please try and help the children. You may wonder how after my death eight weeks ago, you got my letter. Well I worked it out as close as I could, it would take that time for the children to show. I told my solicitor to post this letter eight weeks after my death. This is my final goodbye to you both, God Bless you both, your very grateful and humble friend till the day that we meet again.

Your Friend
Dorothy St Clare.

"Well what do you make of it? She was no fool our Mrs St Clare," said Martin, "but her heart was in the right place, also what good timing with the letter. Shall we let the vicar read the letter?"

"I think we'd better." The next day, Sunday at three o'clock, the vicar turned up. The Powers let him read the letter. They told him all about the children, and told him everything after reading the letter. Listening to the Powers' story he never said a word. Then the vicar stood up and said, "This is well over my head. I cannot help you, but I do know of someone who can. Leave it with me, I'll ring you in a few days' time." By the time the vicar left it was almost nine o'clock at night.

A few days later the vicar rang, "I'm having trouble at the moment getting in touch with my friend, but don't worry, you will meet him." It was almost two weeks to the day when the doorbell rang. Martin opened the door and there standing at the door was an old man, dressed in an old grey pinstripe suit with a dark grey cloak over his shoulders. He had a floppy felt trilby hat on, but its colour was a dark green, black gloves and carrying a black cane with a silver top, it looked like a cat's face on it. The old man said "Mr Martin Powers?"

"Yes," said Martin.

"I'm Mr Smith, I think you and your wife were expecting me."

"Oh yes," said Martin, "Please come in. Jane, Mr Smith is here!"

Martin called to his wife. They told Mr Smith everything and let him read Mrs St Clare's letter. "So you want me to help you with the children, as you say to release them from this world? Well they are not in this world, but caught between two worlds, later I'll explain what I mean." Then Mr Smith got up, "Well, I have to go, thank you both, I will return." and that was that. They watched Mr Smith walked over to an old car and drive away. "Funny, I would have heard his car pull up outside and I don't remember seeing it there when I opened the door! Strange." said Martin, and closed the front door.

It was nearly two weeks later that Mr Smith knocked on the Powers' front door, as soon as Mr Smith was inside the cottage he said "I've first got to tell you both the only way to send the children out of the world they are in to heaven is with help from both of you, and it's a very heavy risk you take, for you both may lose your own mortal life. Go into another room and talk it over on your own, for I cannot help you in any way, it must come from your hearts if you say yes!" So Jane and Martin went into another room, after about 10 minutes they came back and said, "Yes, we will do whatever you want us to do to release the children and help them into heaven."

"Good, thank you both. First thing I want you to do is bring two chairs into the middle of the room and sit down, once you sit down I don't want you to get up out of your chair, whatever you see or hear. Do you both understand?"

"Yes."

"Yes."

"Good. First thing I'm going to do is make a circle round you both. I will walk round the circle three times. I will be inside the circle myself." He then opened a black velvet bag that had strange markings on it, inside the bag was a long dark grey dagger; it also had strange markings on the blade and hilt. He started to walk round in a circle holding the dagger in his right hand straight out in front of him. As he walked round the circle he started to chant to himself in a strange language the Powers had never heard before. As he walked round, coming out of the dagger was a white bright mist of energy, which filled the circle. After going round three times he stopped still. Staying inside the circle he called out.

"HYPNOS GOD OF SLEEP, SON OF NYX, GOD OF NIGHT, COME TO ME, AID ME."

He then called out,

"EARTH, WIND, AIR, FIRE, COME TO ME, AID ME.

"Put Jane and Martin Powers into the outer world of external sleep, let their spirits walk free!" At that very moment the Powers slumped forward in their chairs as if in a deep sleep. Then from their bodies their spirits rose. The Powers in spirit form called out for the children to come to them. As the first child appeared a very bright mist of white energy appeared at the end of the room. Slowly all the children gathered around Jane and Martin. Jane said, "Listen children we are going on a long journey together. When we get to the end of our journey you will never be sad again, for there are lots of other children to play with."

"Are you coming with us?" a little boy asked.

"Yes we're both coming." saying that, Jane took hold of a little girl's hand on her right and a little boy on her left. Martin did the same, "Come, it's time to go." Jane and Martin walked into the light, all the children followed. When the last child had gone into the light the bright white energy went out. Mr Smith, still in the circle, started anticlockwise round the circle he had made, holding the dagger in his left hand, holding it straight out in front of him, again chanting to himself. While he was walking round, the bright energy was returning back into the dagger. On the last circle all the energy had returned and the room was now back to normal. Mr Smith called out,

"THANK YOU, HYPNOS, FOR YOUR HELP AND THANK YOU, EARTH, WIND, AIR, AND FIRE FOR YOUR HELP."

He then blessed the cottage and left.

The next thing the Powers knew was as if they had both fallen out of a tree into a field. But what had really happened is the powers were both asleep, as Martin turned over, so did Jane; she hit him and he hit her with their arms, waking both of them up. He said, "I've just had the strangest dream I've ever had!"

"So have I!" said Jane "What was yours?"

"About an old house and lots of little children."

"That's the same dream I had!" said Martin. She looked at him, but did not say a word. Strange, at last when she spoke "Look at the time Martin! We'll be late for our visit to see Mrs St Clare.

Joseph

Stan Holds was 57 years old, he retired at 55 on medical grounds, he was having heart problems. He said he was sad in a way that he had to stop working for he loved his job. He had been at the post office for over 40 years; he went into the post office from school and that was the only job he ever had. The hospital had told him, "Your life is worth more than your job. If you carry on working it will kill you."

So Stan left the post office. For the next two years Stan just lazed about the house, getting under his wife's feet. One day his wife, Mary, said "Why don't you go buy yourself a dog, then you can go over the park. That will get you out of my way!" Stan liked the idea, so he went to his local pet shop. The pet shop had four puppies; three bitches from one litter and one bitch on her own, she was a funny little thing. As soon as Stan saw her he knew he had to buy her, and it was to be the best buy of his life. So he bought her and took her home.

Within an hour it was as if she had lived there for years. Mary loved her and made a great fuss of her "What are you going to call her Stan?"

"I think I'll call her Joseph, Jay for short."

"But that's a boys' name! Why Joseph?"

"I know it's a boys' name but look how many colours she's got, a bit of black, white, brown, a funny grey and dark red." So it was Joseph, Jay for short from that day on it was said. She was half Alsatian on her mother's side, father unknown. The vet said she will not grow very big, but she was a very healthy puppy.

She had her jabs and Stan was told to keep her in for a few weeks, after that she could go out. Wherever Stan went the little puppy would follow. Stan loved her and you could see the puppy loved Stan, if Stan went into the kitchen and was out there for some time Jay would get up, and go into the kitchen look at Stan then go back into the other room, and the same in the garden;

Stan would go out into the garden and Jay would follow, she would look up at him then lay down, but every now and then would look up at Stan as if to say 'I am keeping my eye on you', making sure he's okay.

It was now nearly a year that Stan had got Jay and he knew Jay was something special, for she knew every word that Stan said to her. Every day they would go over the park, Jay loved the park, Stan would sit on a bench and watch Jay run up and down, but every now and then she would stop and look over, to make sure Stan was okay and still there, and when Stan was not well or the weather was bad Jay seemed to know, and just lay by Stan's feet.

It was the first week in June and the weather was not good, but Stan had the feeling to go over the park – why, Stan did not know, but they went. Now the park is split into two parts, the first part of the park you could park your car, the second part you could not drive into as there was a little bridge with a stream under it to stop the cars going into the main part of the park. On this day there was no one in the park, as the wind was blowing and it look like rain. As Stan and Jay crossed over the little bridge, Jay suddenly ran off down the bank and under the bridge, barking her little head off. No matter how many times Stan called Jay she would not come to him, so Stan went down the bank to see what Jay was up to. He looked under the bridge and could see nothing, but as he went further under the little bridge he saw something small and black. Thinking it may be a rat Stan shouted at Jay "Come here!" and this time she did. Stan moved closer to the little black thing lying in the muddy, dirty stream water under the bridge. When he got quite near, he realised what it was, it was a very small, cold, wet, black kitten.

As Stan picked the little kitten up it meowed at him with a very soft cry. "Poor little thing, come Jay, let's take the kitten home. Mary will know what to do. Good girl." Stan said to Jay and gave Jay a big hug. All the way home Jay kept jumping up and barking. Stan's wife washed the poor little kitten in warm water and used the hairdryer on her. "Lucky Jay found her, I don't think she would have lasted the night. Let's keep her Stan. You've got Jay and I'll have the little kitten. I think I'll call her Lucky."

The vet said the kitten was a little girl and gave Lucky a booster jab. "She'll live." he said as he picked her up and laughed. Lucky had so much food down for her that in the end she just lay down with Jay and went to sleep.

Jay and Lucky became great friends, they would play together, eat together, lie in the garden in the sun together, and even sleep side by side. When Stan had to go to the hospital for a check up or shopping in town and could not take Jay with him, she seamed to know, and a few minutes before Stan would open the front door on his return from the hospital Jay and Lucky would be waiting at the front door for him, so Mary always knew when Stan wood be coming through the door and would put the kettle on.

Stan and Mary had two daughters and four grandchildren. They were always at Stan and Mary's house, for they were a very close-knit family; Stan and Mary loved them and their grandchildren to come over. One Sunday after dinner they were all sitting in the garden, the little three year old girl called Kim was in the garden playing when suddenly Jay jumped up, knocking Kim down, and ran in front of her and started barking at something at the bottom of the garden. Stan knew there was something wrong and ran down the garden. When he got to Jay, he saw not 10 yards away a big brown ugly rat, Stan shouted and the rat ran off at the back of Stan's house where there were fields and a river. Stan said, "That's where the rat came from looking for food. But how did Jay know about the rat? It was about 30 feet away!" They spent the rest of the afternoon talking about Jay and the rat.

This was to be the start of many things that Jay did over the next five years, one day Stan and Mary walked into town. "Let's take Jay on a lead." Stan said. When they were almost in town they had to cross a wide main road, as they went to cross Jay would not move. Stan pulled the lead, "Come on Jay," But the little dog would not move. "You will have to carry her, she may just be frightened of the traffic." But just then a car came round the corner at high speed followed by a police car, as the men in the car had just robbed a factory of its wages. "You know Mary," Stan said "If we had crossed the road we would be dead – we would've been right in the path of that car! I wonder if Jay knew?" he made a fuss of Jay.

About a year later, Stan got a letter from his broker saying his shares are starting to drop, and that he should sell them now, for if they keep dropping he could lose all the money that he had invested, and to let them know. They would post a form for him to sign and return it to them before they could act for him. He rang his broker and they told Stan there was a form already in the post, he should get it the next day, but the next day came and no letter. All week Stan waited for the letter but it never came, so Stan rang again, "But we posted it to you last week, we will post you another form today." For Stan's shares were still falling.

Again he waited all week and still no letter, by now Stan's shares were rock bottom, "It's not worth ringing the brokers, we have lost a lot of money." Stan told Mary. It's was about two weeks later that Stan got a phone call from his broker, "I don't know why you didn't sell your shares, but good job you didn't, they're starting to go up. Don't sell!" Stan was told to wait. A week later Stan got another phone call "Your shares are still going up, If they carry on going up you will be a very rich man!" Three days later, another phone call "Sell now Mr Holder, before they start to drop!" So Stan sold all his shares and made nearly £200,000. Stan now was a rich man.

One morning, about a month later, Stan saw a letter by the front door and sitting by the letter was Jay. Stan picked up the letter and looked at it and the date, it was the letter his broker said he had posted eight weeks ago. Jay got up, looked at Stan, wagged her tail and walked away.

Then there was the time around July, Lucky wanted to go out into the garden, but Jay who was by the back door would not let her pass, and every time Lucky went to run out, Jay would bark at her and Lucky would run back in. Because Stan knew Jay so well by now, almost four years, he felt something was wrong in the garden, He said to Mary "Bet that rat is back in the garden." So Stan got his air gun and went down the garden. At the bottom there was his big, ugly, brown rat, luck was on Stan's side, as the rat did not run off, but just looked at Stan. Stan being a good shot t killed the rat with one shot. "It was that rat again." Stan told Mary "I've just killed it. You know Jay is almost human! God knows what I'd do without her. She's part of my life."

Mary said, "She's certainly part of this family. It would break my heart if we lost her."

In the next year Stan was not a well man, and his days at the park got fewer and fewer. Mary took Jay over the park, but once back she'd go straight to Stan and that's how it was for most of the year. Another story of Jay was one afternoon Stan was reading the paper when there was a knock on the front door. When Stan opened the door a man was standing there. "Sorry to bother you, I've lost my puppy and was told she was last seen down this road. Have you seen her? She's a little Jack Russell."

"Sorry," Stan said "I've been in all day." Jay looked at the man and started to growl. "Stop it Jay. It's alright, she's looking after me." Then next thing Jay ran to the back door and again started to growl and bark then run to Stan, Growling and barking at the man, then again ran to the back door growling and barking. She did this for a good 10 minutes, while Stan spoke to the man. Next thing Stan knew a police car pulled up outside Stan's house.

Two policemen jumped out of the car, ran up the drive to Stan's front door, and grabbed the man. Another police car pulled up, two policemen ran around the back of Stan's house. The next thing Stan knew they were taking another man away, they put him in the police car and drove off. One of the police men came up to Stan "Everything okay?"

"Yes" Stan said "What's that all about?"

"Well sir, it's a con to steal from you, one man knocks, says he lost his dog, while another man goes round the back, comes into your house and steals what he can while his mate keeps you at the front door."

"So that's why Jay kept running to the back door, then to me, she knew someone was out in the garden. Barking all the time!"

"You've got a cleaver dog there." "

Yes and don't I know it! Thank you officer." and the policeman left.

It now got to a stage when Stan was bed-ridden, The doctor said, "He needs plenty of rest." Each week Stan got weaker, but would not go into hospital. Mary wanted him to go but he said, "No I want to be at home with you and Jay." then one afternoon Jay came downstairs, went up to Mary and stayed with her for the rest of the day. It was the first time she has ever done that. The next day she did the same. For two weeks, every afternoon Jay would stay with Mary. Then one morning about eleven o'clock Jay came down the stairs, went up to Mary, looked at her, looked up the stairs, then started howl, a long cold howl, looking up at Mary. "Oh God no!" cried Mary and ran up the stairs to Stan's bedroom. Mary cried out "Stan, Stan, Stan don't go Stan, Stan don't leave me please, Stan don't leave me, Stan!!" But Stan had moved on to another world. The angels had come for Stan.

Mary, holding Stan's hand for a while, went downstairs to phone her two girls and the doctor. She saw Jay looking at her, suddenly a very bright light shone all around Jay, and Jay turned from a little dog into an angel, a beautiful angel. A young beautiful woman with wings smiled at Mary and said "Mary be at peace for Stan is." Then the angel and the bright light were gone, so was Jay. Mary bit her lip and half-cried, then she sat down and cried her heart out. Just before the doctor called Mary said, "I swear to the day I die, I heard Stan call out Jay, it's time to go, Jay. I heard the front door open then close."

Let Me Sing.

Lena Page was born in Northumberland, England in 1974. On the day Lena was born her mother used to tell all her friends she started singing and has not stopped since.

Lena was always singing, by the time she was five years old she knew most of the pop songs. She sang at playschool and anywhere she could. She said, "I just want to sing all the time", and as she got older her voice got stronger; she had a beautiful voice.

At her school, which was a mixed school, her best friend was a boy called John Spencer, she liked being with him, they were always together. She wanted to be a singer and he wanted to be a policeman. By the time Lena was 12 years old she was singing with a local pop group and people came from miles around just to listen to her sing, and by the time she was 15 so many people were asking her to sing that she had to turn a lot of people down. Her mother said she was singing too much. She always asked John, "Shall I sing?"

He would say "Yes." but other times he would say "No." She always trusted him in whatever he said, he was always with her. They were both good at school and both won places at collage and as luck would have it both went to collage at the same time.

It was not long until Lena was singing in pubs and with different pop groups. One day near the end of collage a well known pop group who were not doing very well asked Lena to come and sing at their gig. John was not too happy but said okay, so they went but John felt something was wrong. It turned out that a talent scout was going to be there and with Lena they had a better chance of doing another recording with Lena singing. So after Lena sang two songs John said, "Don't sing anymore, if they want you to sing they have got to pay you £50 for the night". But the pop group did not get offered a recording at the end of collage.

Both doing well John said "Now that collage is almost over what do you want to do next?"

"I still want to sing, but I want to sing as a professional, what do you want to do?"

John said, "I'm going to join the police force, you know Lena, I know someone who has be in the music business for a long time but he has now retired, do you want me to have a word – he may be able to help you?"

So a meeting was set up, Lena liked John's friend straight away, his name was Paul Bernard. "I heard you sing you are very good, you will go right to the top and stay there, do you want me to manage you? This is my deal, sign a five year contract with me, if after one year you want out or I do we will tear up the contract."

"Deal", said Lena.

All three were very happy, Paul was 63 years old and what he did not know about the music world was not worth knowing.

Lena later said to John, "Why did you not say anything about singing contract?"

"I let you do what your hearts told you, you want to sing and Paul will let you sing and make a lot of money".

Paul rang Lena, "You will hear from me in a few days, I'm going to find a song that will blow the roof off the music world, I know just the man but it will take time to get him to write a song, but don't worry."

A week later Paul rang up, "We go and see Peter Morgan tomorrow, bring John with you. He wants to meet you and hear you sing to give him an idea of what kind of song to write for you."

As soon as they met like Paul they hit it off. Peter Morgan said, "It will take about a month to get words and music down."

Paul said, "In the meantime I've got some work lined up for a month so with luck the song could be ready by the time the month is up." and it was.

Peter Morgan rang up and said, "Words and music ready, just waiting for my singer to show up." he laughed and put the phone down.

When Lena heard the song she knew it was her song, it was called *Don't let me wait*.

"I've got a good group ready to record the song with you, it will take a few days to get everything ready, you will have to spend a few days with the group before we make a demo."

A week later everything was ready to make her first recording; it was good, Paul said it was the best but the hardest part would be getting people to play it over the air, but he knew deep down this is what he had been waiting for all his life, he knew Lena was going to be the biggest pop star in the world, he would make sure of that. "I have not spent 45 years waiting for this to let it get away!" he said to himself.

The first DJ he played it to, called Terry May just sat there, he played it once, played it twice and looked at Paul and said, "A star is born, it will be played on my show this afternoon, hold on to your hats it's a number one!"

In fact it was a number one, within four days of the first playing, in less 10 minutes after being played the radio station switchboard was jammed with people wanting to know where they could get the record and the name of the singer.

The group stayed with Lena and they made many hit records. It was the longest number one in the world, and a number one in many countries around the world. Lena was a star overnight.

At the end of the year Paul said to Lena, "The year is up, what do you want to do?"

"I want to sign for life with you, that's if you want me to stay with you since so many people want you to manage them."

Paul said "I told you at the beginning I only want to be *your* manager."

So they signed a life contract and both were very happy. In the next five years Lena had many number one hits and had made a great deal of money, and was the most famous pop star in the world. So many people wanted her on their show, she made three films, many records and travelled all over the world.

By now John Spencer was a police inspector going all over the world on different cases, but he always met up with Lena whenever he could and rang her almost every week or she would ring him. Lots of letters they sent to one another, and never missed one another's birthdays. They were as close as they were the day they first met many years ago.

Lena was in Italy making a film and would be there for four months, and she was doing TV work and a few shows. One day she was sitting outside her flat in Italy in her car when a car hit the back of her car, out got a young, very good looking Italian.

He said "I'm very sorry," and would pay for repair, was she okay, not hurt. Anything he could do for her, could he take her to where she was going"?

Lena drove off, but thinking of the young man a few days later, Lena was shopping when she was knocked and lost her books that fell to the ground, looking to see who knocked her she saw the young Italian. "I'm sorry," he said, "Are you not the lady I hit in my car the other day? I'm so sorry let me pick up your papers and books."

"That's okay," again she said to him.

"Please let me buy you a coffee, it's the least I can do."

"No, that's okay."

"Please let me, my name is Georgio Vellent, just one coffee, please."

"Okay, one coffee."

Lana was pleased he had asked her to have a coffee, she had not had a date for a long time. It was nice to be out having a coffee with a man. They had two coffees and lots of laughs. He told her he was a waiter and asked her what she did. When she told him he said she looked different from photos he had seen of her. As she had to go after two hours, he asked could he see her again. So for the next four months they saw each other nearly every day.

Filming was held up for six weeks, so Lena stayed almost another two months. One day Georgio asked Lena if she loved him, as he was so in love with her, he would think about her and walk into a lamp post. They would both laugh, he made her very happy. She missed him when he could not see her but now she had to leave Italy and leave him behind but could she? No she could not, so she asked him to marry her, but he said, "No, your world is different from mine, you're famous and rich. I'm only a waiter."

But she would not listen, "Do you love me?"

"Yes."

"Do you want to marry me?"

"Yes."

"Then marry me."

"No."

So they spent a night saying 'yes', 'no', 'yes', 'no' but in the morning he said "Yes."

It was a quite wedding, Paul Bernard, his wife, Peter Morgan, his wife, John Spencer, his girlfriend, Terry May DJ, his girlfriend, Lena's group and Lena's family all attended.

At the end of the five years with Paul Bernard, Lena was worth over £30 million and royalties were coming in all the time, she was a very rich lady. Lena came back to England, then they both travelled the world. Lena was singing, recording and filming, every now and then Georgio would fly home to Italy to see his parents who did not go to the wedding as they were both not well enough to travel.

Georgio said one day to Lena, "When we next go on holiday, could we holiday in Italy so I can see more of my parents, I don't think they have long in this world?"

"Yes of course, we can go in October," it was June, "I've got to finish a film, five concerts, and a few shows, then we can go to Italy for as long as you want".

So from June to October Georgio went back to Italy about 10 times to make sure his parents were okay. In October when Lena's work was all finished they flew to Italy, but while in Italy Lena was asked to do a few shows. Georgio was happy for her to do them.

After about a month Georgio said, "What are you doing next Friday?"

"Why?" asked Lena.

"Let's go out shopping for the day in the city, we can have lunch and walk through the park, just you and me, don't tell anyone, we don't want the press to follow us."

Lena loved the idea, so on the following Friday off they went, spending a few hours in and out of the shops, before having lunch, sat in the park, and doing some more shopping. While they were shopping Georgio said, "There is a drug store near here, I've got a headache, let's go to it". So they went to the drug store, Lena wanted to get some things in there. "You get what you want, I'll get my tablets and meet you by the cash desk." They had only been in the store a few minutes when three men burst into the store shouting, "This is a hold up, don't anybody move!"

The cashier tried to hit the first gunman who shot into the air. Hearing the gunman shout and the gunshot, two little girls started to run down the aisle, Lena grabbed them and pulled them to the floor, "Don't say a word", she told them, "Keep quiet."

The mother of the two little girls was in another aisle, also hearing the shot she ran up the aisle shouting "Where are you?" to the two little girls, and as the young woman turned the aisle she was by the cashier and gunman. The gunman, on seeing her, shot her twice, killing her.

Then the police arrived and the gunman started shooting at the police and the police opened fire, killing two of the gunmen. During the shooting Georgio was killed by a police bullet, he was shot in the head and was dead before he hit the ground. Lena was in a terrible state when she found out that Georgio was dead. The gunman was arrested and got life in prison for killing the young woman and for robbery.

Lena did not sing for nearly six months, John Spencer never left her side, he got six months off-duty and they say without him Lena would be dead by now as all she wanted to do was kill herself, but he was there for her and slowly she started to be her old self. Then one day they heard her sing in her bedroom, her first number one; Lena was back, and by nine months from Georgio's death Lena was ready to sing again and do shows.

John Spencer was a very good friend of Inspector Mario Gessppi of Nepal's police force. John had worked alongside Mario Gessppi and had got on very well, both liking one another. Mario's son was getting married and had asked John over to the wedding.

It was now nearly a year since Georgio had been killed, after the wedding Mario said to John "Can you come to my office tomorrow, I want to talk to you about Georgio murder, say about ten o'clock, is that okay?"

"Fine," said John.

So next morning John was at Mario Gessppi's office at ten o'clock. "Thank you for coming, I don't think you will like what I've got to say, but I think I've got it all right. Number one, the gunmen were all friends of Georgio, number two, two of the gunmen came from the next village only 3 miles away, number three, the other gunman came from Georgio's village but moved to another village 15 years ago to get married, he went to the same school as Georgio. Number four, if all three had been killed, I might have not solved it. Number five, lucky for us the one who lived gave me all the clues to the murder and the robbery and number six, why did the gunmen not take any money from the till, there was plenty of money in it? They did not even try, it was that that made me start to look into the robbery.

"The plan was to fake the robbery to kill Lena as if it was an accident, Georgio would get all of Lena's millions, then give his three friends a million each, but instead they killed that young mother, two of them got killed and Georgio, and one got life. Sad, so sad for those two little girls. As I said it did not look right so I started to think of a way to find out more to this case. Then I had an idea, I had an informer doing three years in prison, what if I put him in the same cell as the gunman and got him to start being friendly, he might tell him something about the robbery? Our first break came when one day he said 'I could be living on the French Riviera with millions.' Our second break came again when he said 'Pedro always had big ideas but never had the brain to see them through,' so I checked out Pedro, that was Georgio's nickname as a boy, for all he wanted to do as a boy was fish. Last clue was when he said 'It's 30 days but we do it but we do it in 37 days to make sure?' What did he mean, 30 days but 37days to make sure?"

"I'll tell you," said John, "on the day Lena signed the five year contract they put a clause in the contract, the contract could not become final until after 60 days – the idea was if Lena was killed before 60 days was up the contract became void. They had three meetings inside the 60 days but Paul Bernard was happy and said he could not see anything to stop the contract going through. The five year contract is worth £50 million. I know this is right I was there as a witness for Lena. Lena also told me what she was going to do in her will. Leave half to her family and half to Georgio. But I told her she should leave all she had to her family as they stood by her over the years.

"He also told her 'Do not say anything to Georgio,' and I know she never did, The second part of her will said 60 days after signing the five year contract everything she had was to go to Georgio on her death, this will was done a week before signing. She wanted to buy Georgio a car he always wanted, but it would take up to 30 days to get. The dealers said it was a very hard car to get as not many were made, she wanted it to be a surprise for Georgio. On the day she signed she told Georgio in her excitement, it was 30 days to final contract instead of 60 days. She got mixed up on the two dates, 60 days contract, 30 days car. She told me this the next day, I said 'It doesn't matter, he will be so happy with his new car, don't say anything," so she kept it to herself. Now Georgio put his plan to work, killing Lena on the 37th day, gave him 7 days inside the contract, money safe, but Georgio lost out three times on his plan.

"Number one, lost his life. Number two, lost money he would never have got and number three, would lose his wife, he got his friends to do the robbery by offering a million lira each, all this I can confirm because my friend Paul Bernard was also told about the will and the car."

Mario Gessppi looked at John and said, "Thanks for putting in the missing pieces, I think we can say case closed."

John told Lena everything as he said she had a right to know. Lena asked John why he never asked her out for a date. He told her, "I wanted to ask you out, but you were too good for me."

"And *I* wanted to ask *you* out but you were too good for *me.*"

"I have always loved you Lena."

"And I have always loved you John."

They both laughed and looked into each other's eyes and they both knew tomorrow was the start of a new life.

The Bible

It was 1840 May 20th. Frances Gray was 18 years old. Her grandmother had told her a parcel was on its way for her, with a birthday present. She could not wait for the postman, at last he knocked at her house. Frances could not wait to open the parcel, it was her first birthday present.

"Oh," she said as she unwrapped a small dark blue bible, plus a small box, "what a lovely bible." Inside her grandmother wrote a letter to her, it said:

Dearest Grandchild Frances,

This small bible has been in my family for many years, long before I was born. It was given to me by my father on my 10th birthday, and I have kept it with me through my life. Now that my time is coming to an end, on this birthday I want you to have this bible. It has looked after me and I know it will look after you. Read well of the bible for it will help you in troubled times.

With love to you this day. You will always be in my heart.

Your loving grandmother.

In 1841 Frances met and fell in love with a young soldier who, sad to say, was getting ready to go to war. Then the day came and he had to say goodbye to Frances. He asked Frances to wait for him, for when he came back from the war he would asked her to marry him. She wanted to give him something to take with him to remember her by, so she gave him her grandmother's bible, saying "This bible will keep you safe so that you will return to me."

When he opened the bible he started to read a verse but the rest of the verse was so badly faded, it was impossible to read. Frances told him that it was a very old bible and no one knew what the rest of the verse said, all you could read was:

'They that please the lord God, shall go their way in peace.'

"I want you to give me the bible back when you come home", said Frances.

"I will, I will", said the soldier. Not knowing Frances would marry him, this bible they would marry on, on his return.

So the young soldier went off to war to fight in a far off land, standing in the trenches the soldiers were waiting to go over the top. The officer said, "When I blow my whistle, go". Before he knew it the officer had blown his whistle and the men were starting to go over the top. Up and over he went, he had not gone more than 100 yards when he knew no more.

He woke up in a field hospital, a doctor looking down on him, "How do you feel, you are a very lucky soldier; the bible you had in your top army jacket saved your life, for the bible took the bullet that was meant for you. I've never seen anything like this in all my years as a doctor."

The young soldier returned home after the war and married Frances, they lived a very long and happy life, having four children. Frances put the bible away, they moved house because of the children and somehow the bible got lost.

Frances' grandmother died six months after giving the bible to Frances, and poor Frances never got over losing her. Her other present was a ladies' silver watch.

In 1864 the bible was found in an old wooden box at the back of an old shed, how it got their no one knows. It was found by a man who lived by stealing anything he could get his hands on, his wife and his son stole from anyone they could, then sold whatever they got to live on, but most of the money went on drink; they were a bad lot. He took the old box home with him, inside the box were plates, a silver teapot, a small silver boy, old photos, old papers and the small bible.

"Here woman!" he called out, "Sell this for food and wine." But he took the bible out of the old box and threw it into a cupboard and left it there, but before doing so he looked through the bible and read the verse and laughed at it, and the bible was forgotten.

In 1864 another great war started and men were called up to go and fight, The bad man's son was called up.

The bad man, three months after finding the bible, died in terrible pain. The mother put a few things into an old case for her son to take with him, the bible was already in the case so the mother did not bother to take it out.

Like the father the son was bad, always fighting, stealing and drunk and had been to prison many times. Again waiting in the trenches to go over the top the bad soldier stood, next to another soldier who said to him "Thank you for letting me read your bible, here it is."

"I don't want it, it's no good to me, you can have it."

The officer called out, "Stand by to go over the top."

The soldier put the bible in his pocket, then they were sent over the top. The soldier was one of the first to be hit, the bad man got nearly 200 yards when he got shot in the head and was dead before he hit the ground.

The other soldier lived, but was sent home, his days of fighting were over and he lived for many years.

The mother of the bad soldier, on hearing of her son's death, drunk herself to death.

The soldier kept the bible for many years and often told friends about the bad soldier and the bible. When the soldier's own son was 18 years old, he went to join the Royal Navy in 1903. The father gave the bible to his son. "This bible will keep you safe while you're away at sea."

The ship that the sailor joined had to escort merchant ships to countries the other side of the world, who were at war for two and half years. The sailor sailed round the world carrying food supplies and at one time his ship was turned into a hospital ship. It was on his last trip when the ship was on her way home that it was attacked by enemy planes.

The first attack killed many men and injured many more, the second attack damaged the ship, but it could still sail home. The last attack made a large hole in the side of the ship, then the planes were gone.

The sailor did not get home through the raids, but one of the magazine holes was right by the hole in the ship, the magazine exploded sending pieces of metal all over the place, again killing more sailors. One piece of metal hit the young sailor in the leg and he fell badly injured, he was rushed to the ship's hospital. The doctor has to do a very quick operation to save his life. The doctor came to see him, shook his head and said, "You are a very lucky man, you still have both your legs, if it was not for the bible in your trouser pocket you would have lost your leg, but the bible is in a terrible mess, covered in blood and most of the pages are missing, but I am sorry to say your navy days are over, you will be able to walk again but not for a very long time." He continued "You know I've never seen a bible like that before, most bibles would never hold out like your one did against flying metal."

The sailor did not want to give up the bible but because the doctor had saved his leg and his life he gave him the bible.

"What do I need it for now? No one can read it, it's full of torn missing pages and covered in blood."

After returning home he had to rest up, 6 months later he was up and walking about. One afternoon he went to cross the road in front of a bus when his leg gave way and he fell under the bus and was killed.

In 1909 the doctor died in his sleep, about a year later the doctor's wife was looking for some papers to do with the doctor. She had Beth, her granddaughter staying with her. She could not find what she was looking for so Beth said "There is only one place left to look – in grandfather's little black doctor's case."

When she found it and opened it up there were the papers she was looking for and also an envelope; inside the envelope was the little badly torn and bloody bible. She went to take out the bible saying, "So this is the bible he talked about so many times." But it fell out of her hands onto the floor in many tiny pieces. The little girl went to pick it up but the grandmother said, "Leave it Beth, I'll go and get a dustpan and brush", and the grandmother left the room.

Beth picked up the torn, blood-soaked pages from the bible. There was one page that was covered in blood with a hole, and through the blood Beth could see the writing starting to come through in black ink, and the little girl could read what was written. But at that moment her grandmother came back into the room and the piece of bible page fell to pieces through her fingers.

This is what the writing said in the little dark blue bible:

They that please the Lord God
Shall go their way in peace.

The grandmother, Frances Gray, the first soldier, the bad man, his wife, the son, the second soldier, the army doctor, the navy doctor and many other people over the years who read or who had possession of the bible could read the verse but no one could read the other verses as they were badly faded, but the little girl could and this is what she read.

But they who anger the lord God,
Will feel the wrath of the lord God.
In the year of our Lord
1609.

Then under that was written.

For only the eyes of a child can read the ways of the Lord God.

The Last Train.

It all started at a friend's wedding reception, that's when I saw him for the first time, standing just inside the hall door. He just stood there watching everyone having a great time, the music was loud, plenty of food and free drink, lots of people dancing. I was talking to my brother, I don't know what made me look over to the hall door, it may have been because a lot of people had just turned up that I noticed him.

I had never seen him before, he was about 45 to 50 years old, in a grey suit, about 6 foot tall, he had a small beard. In an odd way he was a good looking man. He seemed to be looking for someone, he then found who he was looking for and walked over to two old ladies sitting on chairs; to get to them he had to pass me and as he did he looked at me and smiled and gave a small nod. When he reached the two old ladies he just stood there looking at them.

Then it happened, one of the old ladies suddenly fell forward off her chair onto the floor, people rushed over to her. One of the first to get to her was Doctor Jim Martin, brother of the bride. Standing by the stranger, he bent down to see what he could do, looked up and said "I'm sorry but she is dead!" I found out later that the old lady was Mrs Mary Bell, the groom's father's sister. Then as the doctor stood up it happened, coming out of Mrs Bell's body was a glowing bright white light, the stranger took Mrs Bell's hand, they both looked at me, smiled, turned and walked away through the wall of the hall and was gone, so was the bright light.

I just stood there looking at the wall they both had gone through, then at the dead body lying on the floor, the body of Mrs Mary Bell.

Had I just witnessed the Angel of Death who had come for Mrs Bell? I've seen films of angels coming for people, read books and once went to see a play called *The Angel from Heaven*. Now I'd seen it for real, an ambulance was called and soon afterwards the party broke up, a happy day turned sad. I asked a few people if they saw the stranger but all said no, was I the only one who saw him? And if so why me?

It took some time to get over what I saw but after a while I was back to my old self. Then I saw him again, it must have been just over two years later. I was waiting at the school bus stop for my son, there were a lot of people waiting near the bus stop; I looked round to see if I knew anybody and that was when I saw him. Again he looked at me then started to walk towards the road, I watched him, who was going to die, who was he waiting for? As he passed me he smiled and gave a small nod, then suddenly I heard a squealing of breaks, followed by a heavy thud, a taxi had hit a man who had run across the road from behind a bus.

From where I was standing I could see a man lying in the road, and standing by him was the strange man. The dead man started to leave his body, a very bright white light was all around him, they looked over at me, smiled and then started to walk away through a lorry that had stopped, and then they were gone.

That night I could not sleep. Why was I the only person who could see the angel, see the dead person leave their body, and walk away into the emptiness? Was the stranger an angel? I called him the Angel of Death, but who was he, was this a warning of some kind? Lots of things went through my mind, but none made sense. Did I have special powers of sight, could I see the dead when no one else could? Should I go and see the vicar? I decided not to, I'd wait and see if it happened again – and it did.

I had to go for a medical for a new job, while I was waiting to see the doctor a man came in, gave his name and sat down next to me. He must have only sat down for two minutes when the nurse came over and told him to go to room 12A, it was about five minutes later that the nurse came out, walked over to the phone and I heard her say, "Can you send an ambulance?"

Then a very bright white light shone by room 12A and I saw my friend with the man looking over at me, both smiled, turned and walked through the wall and were gone.

I found out the man was Mr Paul Bayamon, a very rich and powerful man in the city who only popped into the surgery for a quick chat with his friend Doctor Benton. He was 54 years old.

It was now three years since the last time I saw the Angel of Death. In my new job I had to go to lots of meetings for the company and many of then did not finished until late. This last meeting did not finish until one in the morning, normally I would stay in a hotel for the night but I had to get home as that day I started my holidays and had left my car in a car park by the station. I got to the station at 1.15am, the last train Bramoor Heath was 1.30am, so I had plenty of time, I sat down to wait for the train. I looked up and down the platform, no one else was waiting for the train, only me. I looked at the station clock, it was one of those clocks that tell you when the train will be coming into the station; it was 1.20am, 10 minutes to the train.

I got fed up of sitting down and walked to the end of the platform. I walked back to the clock, it was 1.26am, only four minutes. I looked down the platform, there was one person waiting, three minutes to go. The person was a man, he started to walk towards me, I looked at the clock and there were two minutes to go. The man was halfway up the platform, I looked at him – oh no! It was the Angel of Death, one minute left, I could hear the train not very far off, he was only 20 yards away.

The train came into the station, he had almost reached me, the train stopped, I walked up the platform away from him, the doors opened and as I went to get into the carriage inside I looked back quickly, he was right by my side, then looked into the carriage, and cried, "Oh God no!"

The Piano Player.

Our story starts in Berlin, Germany in 1925, Leah Stienbury was five years old. Her mother and father both worked at the Berlin Collage of Music. Leah's parents had both been piano teachers, but because of a bad fall her father could not use his left arm and could no longer teach. He used to teach the piano and the violin, but now was on the board of examiners for piano and violin, and he gave lectures at the collage. Leah was listening to her mother play a piece of piano music that she had not played for some time. She would play the music then stop and start again, "It's no use, I'll have to go and get the music, I just cannot get the last part of this piece!" So she left the room. As soon as Leah's mother had left the room Leah went to the piano and started to play the music her mother had just played. Her mother stood by the door, and called out to her husband, "Come and listen to Leah play the piano!"

"Where did you learn to play like that?"

"I listen to Mother play then when she is not here I play on the piano." On that day a genius was born.

In the next 15 years Leah played the piano and passed her highest and final exam when she was 20 years old. Over 15 years Leah built a very high reputation and was asked to play many times in and out of Berlin. It was not long before the German High Command got to hear about Leah and she was asked to play at cocktail parties where generals, brigadiers and captains would be and they would sit down and listen to her play. One night she was playing for the High Command when the Führer turned up with a party and after her playing she was introduced to the him. From that night on she was a very important person in Berlin and the whole of Germany.

In 1939 war came and Germany went to war, marching into Poland, then England came into the war and Europe. Adolf Hitler wanted to take on the rest of the world.

In 1939-1940 the Gestapo started to round up all the Jews in Germany and Poland and they were taken away, many were killed and many were never seen again. Then one day Leah was told the Gestapo had gone to the collage and taken all the Jews away. When she heard this she went to the High Command building in Berlin pleading for their release, "I'll do anything for Germany if you don't harm them, and let them go!" After filling forms in and spending most of the day at the building she was told to come back in a week's time at 10am to room nine. One week later Leah was back at the High Command building, she was told not to speak but to follow a guard out of the building to a waiting car. She was taken to the headquarters of the Gestapo a few miles outside Berlin to a prison called Loufant. The prison was now being used by the German Intelligence; prisoners went in and were never seen again. Leah was taken down to the basement, to a cell that was now being used as an office.

An intelligence officer was waiting, a Captain Hirink. He told her to sit down, "Do not smoke or speak, and when the colonel comes in to stand up, only answer questions put to you." Leah sat there for over an hour before the colonel arrived with two other people, one a woman in plain clothes, and the other a small man in a black suit, very small glasses and a briefcase. The colonel sat down, the small man sat at a small table, and the woman stood by Leah. Captain Hirink stood behind the colonel, both the colonel and Captain Hirink wore Lugers. Outside the cell a two man guard stood, both armed with small machine guns. The little man looked at Leah then at the colonel who nodded. and the little man said, "Only answer 'yes' or 'no' to my questions. Do you understand?"

"Yes."

"Good. You were born on the 16th May 1920?"

"Yes."

"In the Central Hospital Berlin, a Jewish Hospital?"

"Yes."

"You are the only child of Eriea and Henrick Steinburg?"

"Yes."

"Eriea and Henrick Steinburg, both musicians who teach at the Berlin Collage of Music?"

"Er…"

"Yes or No?"

"Yes."

"Good. Your parents are in Arkua Jail yes?"

"I don't know where they are!" At that the meeting was over, Leah found out that the little man was Doctor Oan Vonja. During the meeting Leah noticed that the phone rang five times but no one went to answer it, they just looked at the phone while it rang. There was one more question after the phone rang and it was over. "You may now go but I want you back here in one week's time. Do not tell anyone of this meeting, carry on as you normally do. Do you understand?"

"Yes."

"Good. Go to the High Command building in Berlin to room 131, at 10 am a car will take you to the bus station there, once you're there get a bus back into Berlin."

"Yes, yes."

A week later Leah was standing outside room 131, she stood there for nearly two hours then she was called into the room and was told to sit down, not to smoke or speak, and to stand up when the colonel entered the room, then the guard left. It was a very large room with very thick carpet, and a long table with nothing on it. Behind the table was very big painting of the führer and a very high and long window that overlooked a well-kept garden. Suddenly the two great doors at the other end of the room opened and in came the colonel followed by Dr Oan Vonja and an army major. Leah stood up, when they were all seated Leah was told to come to the table and sit in the only empty chair, but this time Doctor Oan Vonja was speaking to her in a nice friendly voice, calling her 'Leah', "Would you like some tea or something to eat?"

"No thank you."

"Good, let's get on and tell you why you are here. If you co-operate your mother and father will come to no harm, you said you would do anything for the führer and country, yes?"

"Yes."

"Good, two nights a week you will play the piano on the Berlin radio to our troops and to the enemies of our führer, you will work with Major Volks.

"Major Volks is also a fine musician like yourself, so you will work together, yes?"

"Yes."

"Good, your music will be coded, our people in England will also hear your music; we plan to send our first broadcast of your music in three weeks' time, so you have a lot to do, yes?"

"Yes."

"Good, we will meet in three days' time." Leah wondered how coded messages could go over the air just from her playing the piano. For the next three days Leah played her music, Major Volks just listened and now and then put something down on paper. At the start Major Volks said to Leah, "You will call me 'Major' at all times do you understand?"

"Yes."

"Good now let us start." So three days later Leah again sat in front of the colonel, Dr Oan Vonja and the major. Again Dr Oan Vonja was nice to her, "How is your health?"

"Fine."

"How is your music?"

"Fine."

"Good, very good, is there anything you need?"

"No."

"Good, as from today you will not leave the building, you will live here, you will only speak to Major Volks and the people you work with. Do you understand?"

"Yes."

"We will meet again in three days for our final meeting. Meeting over!"

Major Volks said to Leah "I have news for you about your broadcast, you will do eight broadcasts, Tuesday night for half an hour, 8-8.30pm, Thursday night for half an hour, 9-9.30pm As I find out more I'll let you know."

At the final meeting Dr Oan Vonja said, "I have some papers for you to sign and a few more questions. First are you of Jewish blood? Second are your mother and father Jewish?"

"Yes, yes."

"Good. You, your mother and father are German Jews?"

"Yes."

"Good that's all the questions I wish to ask. Now come and sign these forms. They are to release your parents, to say that you are Leah Steinburg and that you play the piano to broadcast for Germany and for the führer and for all German people to listen to you play. I will enjoy!" Dr Vonja said. So the last meeting was over Dr Vonja said "I have a message for you, it's from the führer himself, he said he is looking forward to hearing you play for him again. It is a great honour for you Leah." Dr Vonja also said "And your mother and father will leave jail, they are fine and well and you will soon meet them again"

After they had all left Major Volks said "Leah I have news for you, as you know you will only do eight broadcasts, after that you will have a short rest.

Over in England a few weeks later at British Intelligence in Whitehall, London, by a stroke of luck one officer was speaking to another who was asked, "How are you doing? Are you ready to sit your exam?"

"Do you know," the officer said "I found an old code book; it said England was one of the first countries to send messages by code, by music in the 18th century.

"In France during the French Revolution playing the harpsichord would give messages to British spies, help would come, helping people get to England, the code used then was Maria!" At that he walked off, then stopped and said, "Wouldn't it be funny if that Germany woman Leah Steinburg was sending messages over to England or another country by playing the piano? But I don't think so, you know she is Jewish, see you later!" Off he went. As the officer was walking back to his office it hit him, he got to his office and rang room. 721 and within 10 minutes he was telling his story to his commanding officer John Dangerfield, head of operations. "I think we may be onto something, get me all you can on this Steinburg woman, dates, times she plays and all recordings of her. When is she playing next?"

"Tomorrow night 9-9.30pm Sir." Within a few hours John Dangerfield had lots of paperwork on his desk "Of Leah Steinburg, it will be her seventh broadcast, she is doing a set of eight Sir."

"I want six men on this, put then to work right away and any more you may need. I want them to work round the clock. When was her last broadcast?"

"26th October 1940 Sir. If she is coding her music who or what are they after?"

Dangerfield said, "Churchill Sir."

"No, why do you say Churchill?"

"Well Sir he will be in Egypt from the 26th October until the 30th."

"Where about in Egypt?"

"Cairo. As we know Sir, Leah is doing her last broadcast on the 20th then having a short rest."

"If she is coding her music to kill Churchill that gives the Germans four days to plan. Get everything ready for the eighth broadcast; it will tell them where and when to strike and six days to get in and kill Churchill before we know it."

"Clever, very clever – that's if you're right Mason!"

Leah's broadcast was studied by Dangerfield's men; they worked round the clock and little pieces started to fall into place – or did they? On Leah's eighth broadcast it just did not make sense, but there was something there, on each of her broadcasts she had to play four pieces of music, and talk to the troops. Major Volks spoke most of the time telling the German people that Germany was, and would, win the war and telling the troops the führer was there for them all, and after the war was won, Germany would honour it's people, Germany would rule the world.

After Leah's eighth broadcast she went to see her parents, who were well and living in the country, for plans were being made to get them out of Germany. It had been raining hard for almost a week with cold strong winds. One evening Leah went to the pictures and saw the last show, coming out of the pictures at about 10pm. It was still raining heavily and was getting colder; as Leah got near to her flat she had to cross the road. It was dark as the road was by a small park, as she started to cross the road a car pulled away from the kerb, Leah had no chance to get out of the road. She had her head down against the strong wind and rain and was hit head on and killed outright. She lay in the road for five minutes before an old man found her. The car did not stop.

Other Points

Did the Germans set up British Intelligence?
Did they know code Maria, France 18th century or were they going to kill Churchill but were stopped?
Did they know all the code, half the code?
While British Intelligence worked on Leah did the Germans get who they were after or what?
We will never know!
Why does no one know the name of the German Colonel that Leah met at least four times at meetings with Dr Vonja?

Germany Facts As We Know Them

Leah did broadcast eight times to the troops and German people in 1940.

Leah was killed by a car.

The Germany of the 1940s was ruled by Adolf Hitler.

The Germans hated the Jewish people.

The Gestapo hated the Jewish people.

Adolf Hitler hated the Jewish people.

There was 82nd commando force called Night Raiders.

Leah was Jewish.

So were her parents.

OTHER FACTS

Germany lost the war and surrendered in 1945.

No one knows what was going on in Leah's head before she was killed.

We do not know who killed Leah; German agents or British. Or was it an accident? If it was why did the driver not stop, or did he? And not call the police?

Leah's parents – what happened to them?

Why would the German High Command say they have nothing to say but were looking into her death?

Was Leah playing coded music on her broadcast?

Was she a willing party to kill Churchill by playing, or did she play to save the lives of her parents?

Is there a file on Leah Steinburg in a vault somewhere in Germany?

Was there a general called Strolrik, a doctor called Oan Vonja, a major called Volks, a Captain Hirink and a nameless colonel?

Were there two coded letters found, one on the 5th May 1940, the second 18th June 1940 but no one will say where, when or by who?

Where did the leak come from? Where the letters were found by

British Intelligence ?

The first letter was dated 5th May 1940.

From High Command Headquarters Berlin.

Operation Victory code 2 0 8 1 0 0

Date 24/10/40-30/10/40

Unite 82 Commando Force (Night raiders)

Signed by:

General Strolrik

Commanding Office

Operations North Africa

Second letter found date 18/10/40

Operation Victory code 2 0 8 1 0 0

Night sky clear

Signed by:

General Strolrik

Commanding Officer

Operation North Africa.

These two letters came to light, a phone call, each letter read out, date of phone call not given.

There was a music code France 18th century British Intelligence have in under Code 0 2 9 0 (Maria)

The Germans did send coded messages over the radio, as did the British and the rest of the world.

Why did British Intelligence record all Leah's broadcasts?

Was there a British Officer who told John Dangerfield Germany may be planning to kill Churchill?

There was a John Dangerfield, head of British Intelligence.

Did the Germans kill Leah's parents or did British agents kill her to stop them from talking?

Again was there a Maria code France 18th century

Did Leah know she was being used and that they might kill her after her last broadcast as she knew to much and she was a Jew?

Is there a file on Leah Steinburg somewhere in the vault in England?

We know Churchill stayed prime minister throughout the war and brought victory and peace to the world.

There was a Leah Steinburg who played the piano in Germany in the 1940s and who played for Adolf Hitler, but what we do not know is if this is a true story or fiction?

Perhaps one day Leah Steinburg will play her music again, and tell her story.

The Storm

Because of the 1932 Royal Navy Secrecy Act (S1 6148 shipping information file DR42C) I cannot give the place, year, names or ship but I can write this story using a different title to a true story. But not a true story! By using true names, places and year I could go to prison for five years so I've called this story *The Storm.*

My story starts on the 22nd April 1983 somewhere in the Caribbean Sea, the destroyer HMS Reptile was patrolling looking for smugglers and pirates that trafficked drugs, guns, stolen goods and human beings. There were many in these waters operating illegally and it was the job of the Royal Navy to capture or sink these boats.

HMS Reptile was a destroyer of the Manchester class guided missile type (42C) batch 3. Her captain was Captain Henry Lloyd York and his number one was Simon Charles Brentock, whose nickname aboard ship was Jimmy. At about 11.15am it was reported to the captain that a large cruiser was 10 miles off the destroyer starboard bow. "Let's take a look – full ahead!" he ordered.

Jimmy told the captain "I'm sure it's the sea runner I've seen pictures of her."

"Good, thank you number one." So the destroyer turned into the wind in full pursuit. Messages were sent to the cruiser to heave to but she turned and started to make a run for it.

The destroyer could do 33 knots. At 11.30am it was clear that the cruiser was losing the race against the destroyer. "Put a shot across her bows and send a message that if the sea runner does not heave to I'll sink her!" So a message was sent and a shot was put across her bows, the sea runner cut her engines dead. "Slow ahead" Captain York said "I've waited a long time to catch the sea runner." On board the destroyer were 15 Royal Marines under the command of Major Alec Paul Wyper. Major Wyper's number one Lieutenant David Knight was told to "Stand to the Marines, tell Sergeant Marshall I want a word with him."

"Yes Sir."

"You want me Sir?" the sergeant asked.

"Yes Sergeant, we board the sea runner as soon as we come along side." The marines were very highly trained to do almost anything. Five hundred tons of solid, battle-grey steel coming at you it must be a formidable sight and anyone wanting to take the British destroyer would have to be stupid or as powerful as the destroyer. He would have to have a good chance of beating the war ship. The British war ship carried 450 ships' company, 4.5 automatic gun port and automatic starboard Gatling gun, two sets of torpedo tubes, eight mark 46 torpedoes, four harpoon missiles for land and enemy shipping, one helicopter, a Lynx which carries a four man crew, door-mounted machine gun 7.62 calibre, general purpose machine gun GPMG, sea skua ant shipping missiles plus two depth charges and as I said, top speed of 33 knots.

The marines quickly boarded the sea runner and arrested the captain, a Greek Captain Apakopalise who was wanted around the world. The marines found many cases of drugs, cases of guns, and cases of electrical goods and 134 men and woman being smuggled into Jamaica. The sea runner was escorted back to Kingston Port and handed over to the Jamaican port authorities, and the captain was arrested and taken to prison on smuggling charges; he could go to prison for a very long time. The HMS Reptile returned to Kingston, Rear Admiral Anderson St Clare was in Kingston on a very important meeting with Royal Navy High Command. He was a very good and close friend of Captain York so when he heard that the destroyer HMS Reptile was in port he sent a message so he and his friend could meet for dinner at eight o'clock at the officers' club.

It was a good night for both of them, for it had been over a year since they last met and had lots to talk about. It was past two o'clock when they parted company, but neither knew they would never meet again. In his report Captain York wrote that the sea runner was smuggling drugs, guns, people and stolen goods through the Caribbean, running from Cuba, Dominican Republic, Haiti and Jamaica and now he had been captured it would make smuggling much harder as the sea runner was a large cruiser and fast and knew the seas very well, and knew when and where the British Navy would be. They would make sure they were in another part of the sea but for some reason the sea runner was in the wrong place at the wrong time and as a result was captured.

On the 29th April HMS Reptile left Kingston port to resume patrolling the Caribbean Sea. While in port the destroyer refuelled and took on fresh water stores and had a few jobs done on board. Ten of the crew left the ship, and 10 new crew joined, plus the ship's doctor left and was replaced. On the 3rd May 10.20am Captain York was told that bad weather was ahead, and within 30 minutes the skies were getting very dark. It started to rain heavily and the winds were very strong, lighting streaked across the sky with heavy thunder. The sea got very rough with a very heavy swell – it was a very bad storm. It was almost black and the skies suddenly seemed to open as if a gap was appearing; the gap was a very pale dark orange and yellow. It got bigger, the lighting was now continuous.

The captain watched the storm from the wheel house. The ship was heading into the storm, it dipped and rolled while the captain watched the gap in the sky. The very pale dark orange and yellow sky now seemed to get bigger but it was still very dark. Just for a moment the captain thought that the pale dark orange yellow sky was slowly merging with the sea and that he saw a large what look like galleon fall into the sea. Then a few minutes later the rain stopped and so did the wind, the skies started to light up, the sea was calm, gone was the lighting and thunder, and a few minutes later it was back to a hot sunny day.

The boson said to Captain York, "I've been at sea for 26 years and I've never seen a storm like that before. It was a bad one, I did not know they had storms like that in the Caribbean."

"Nor did I, I would not have believed it if I hadn't seen and been in one."

On the 6th May 10.20am it was reported to the captain that what looked like a large galleon had suddenly appeared on the port bow. "I checked and it's not on radar."

"So where did it come from?"

"Don't know Sir, one minute it was not there then it was." the third officer said, "For a hobby I read a lot on galleons and it looks as if it as big as Nelson's Victory."

"How far off is it?"

"Six to 8 miles."

"Right let's take a look." So the destroyer turned hard to port; the captain look up at the sky, "Oh no it looks like another storm coming up." and he was right for the wind had started to pick up. It began to get dark then it started to rain, and then the sea started to get a heavy swell and a few minutes later lighting streaked across the sky. Thunder crashed, it was almost like nigh;t it was a bad storm and the destroyer was heading right into it. Suddenly the sky started to break open and a large gap appeared.. A very pale dark orange/yellow sky appeared, it looked like the yellow sky was falling into the sea. The galleon was heading into the yellow sky and the destroyer was following. The large galleon was only about 4 miles off, "I don't think we can board her in this weather." the marine major told his sergeant, "Leave the Gemini dinghy below and stand down the marines." A message was sent to Kingston reporting the galleon the bad storm. The time of the last message received from the destroyer was 11.05am.

Kingston sent many messages but got no answer. Rear Admiral Anderson St Clare said, "If I did not know Captain York I would say he was having a break down – very heavy storms, a galleon in the Caribbean, what next?" But the destroyer was not heard or seen of again, "Read me the last message from the destroyer."

"Heading into a very bad storm in pursuit of a galleon." The Rear Admiral shook his head and walked away, stopped and looked back, "Is the radio officer 100% sure it was HMS Reptile?"

"Yes Sir."

He shook his head again, "Thank you." and walked off. A rescue sea plane was sent out to search for the destroyer and the destroyer Courage was also sent out to look for the lost destroyer but the sea plane reported, "No sightings." It was sent out many times and each time no sightings were reported, also the Courage reported no sightings.

The rear admiral said, "How could Captain York report a storm when our weather officer could find no storm anywhere in the Caribbean seas? Very strange, very strange!" The destroyer Courage was told to take over patrolling the Caribbean seas.

Date 17th May, time 10.25am. It was reported to Captain Roger Martin that a galleon was on the port side about 10 miles away. "It must be the Galleon that Captain York saw. Send a message reporting the sighting of the galleon, give our position"

"Yes sir." so the destroyer Courage headed towards the galleon. "Captain?"

"Yes?"

"It looks like a storm coming up fast." and in the next five minutes the skies grew very dark, the wind was very strong with a very high sea swell, thunder and lighting ripped across the sky.

The storm got worse as the destroyer headed into it, suddenly the sky started to break open and a large gap started to form, and a very dark pale orange/yellow sky appeared. It looked as if the yellow sky was falling into the sea and the galleon was heading for it. At 11.10am the last message received from the Courage said, "Following Galleon into storm: storm very bad."

The radio officer said, "Oh no not again!" and reported it to Rear Admiral St Clare. They tried many times to contact the destroyer Courage but she never answered. Once again the sea plane was sent out, the Frigate Torn was also sent out but the destroyer was never seen or heard of again. "This is really strange." the Rear Admiral "Very, very strange." and from that day the Galleon was never seen again and all Royal Navy ships were told to report, but not follow if the galleon was sighted. This case is still on file, awaiting conclusion.

The Tea Pot Fairies

Old Mary White was an 87 year old widow, she still did her own shopping, cleaning, washing and loved doing her little garden. Her husband had died three years ago: her two daughters Pat and Jean had wanted her to sell her house and move in with her youngest daughter Jean, but she said, "No, I've lived in this house for 67 years. I moved in on my wedding day, when I was 20. It holds lots of beautiful memories for me. By living here I feel your father is near me. You two girls were born in this house and you both grew up here, plus most of my friends live nearby and my little club is just round the corner. I want to live here until I die. If I move your father might not know were to find me when it's my turn to go." No matter what they said her answer was always 'no, no, no and no.'

She walked to the shops almost every day with her friend Mini de la Rue. Mini was born in France and she married a British soldier and moved to England, but sad to say her husband died through injuries he got in the war. They were only married for 10 years. Three or four times a week her two daughters would call round to see her and make sure she was okay, and if there was anything they could do or anything she wanted; money-wise Mary was well off. The two girls would fuss over her for they loved her very much. She would say "For God's sake you two, leave me alone. If you want to do something go and make a cup of tea!"

And they loved it and would say, "What are we going to do with you?" and would all bust out laughing, and she in turn loved them for her life was built around her two daughters and four grandchildren.

She was always buying them things and was always being told off by her two daughters. Her friend Mini, (de la Rue was her nickname at the little club they belong to, for Mini was born in an avenue called de la Rue she would say "I lived in de la Rue

I did this in de la Rue I did that in de la Rue. I met my husband in the avenue de la Rue I worked in de la Rue…" and because she kept on about France they at their club nicknamed her Mini de la Rue) was a good friend to Mary and they were always in one another's homes, plus Mary's daughters made a lot of fuss of her. She made many friends.

Mary had just got home from her daughters' as she went to their home every Thursday, when the doorbell rang. It was her friend Mini, "Hello, what are you doing here? You know it's Thursday."

"Yes but I just popped over to see you, I've got you a little present."

"But you are always doing things for me!" So over a cup of tea Mini told her all about the present "Stan, my oldest boy, rang me this morning and asked if I would like to go to town with him, he has to see some people and it would only take an hour, then he would take me for a meal, so I jumped at it. While he was seeing these people I went for a walk round the shops. I passed an old junk shop so I went in to looked around."

"What, the old junk shop by the post office?"

"Yes,"

"I know it."

"Well, I looked around and right at the end of the shop are some shelves, and on one of them I saw…I won't tell you – you will have to open the box. I liked them straight away thinking of you, the man said they were in a set of six so I bought the set for you. I hope you like them. He told me they were made in Ireland round about 1920 in or near Kerry. He had them for a very long time and could not sell them. I think to get rid of them he sold them to me at half price. I think I got a good deal." Mary opened the box and inside there were six teapots, and on each one there was a lid with a little fairy in a different position on each lid, all the teapots were a creamy white colour. On each there were flowers and they also had six different markings on them. One had a butterfly, two had a ladybird, three had a dragonfly, four had a bluebird, five had a honey bee and six had a moth. They were beautifully painted in blue, yellow, white, red, pale green, and mauve. They were about three inches by two inches round.

All the little fairies on the lids were painted in different colours, and all had tiny wings also painted in different colours. To Mary they were beautiful; she loved them as soon as she saw them. Mini said, "The man said they needed washing in soapy water, they are made of Irish clay."

Mary said "Thank you Mini, that's the best present you could ever buy me. I'm going to wash them and put them along my mantelpiece so everyone will see them." When Mini went home Mary was so happy with her present that she rang her two daughters and told them. That night Mary washed her six little teapots in soapy water very gently. They came up like new, she dried them and as she put them on her mantelpiece she said "I love every one of you." That night Mary found it very hard to sleep and even got up in the night to go down and look at her six fairy teapots.

The next day by ten o'clock both daughters were at Mary's house to see the fairy teapots. They both loved them Jean said, "You know Mum, fairies bring you luck and you've got six lots of luck." Then there was a knock at the door, it was Mini and for the next two hours the four of them talked about nothing but the six teapots and fairies. That afternoon Mary and Mini went to the local library and got four books on fairies, and the rest of the day was spent reading all about fairies. That night again Mary could not sleep, for now she knew lots about fairies, but at last she fell asleep. In the next few days she found herself talking to her six little fairy teapots.

It was three nights later when Mary went to bed, only to be woken up by something at about one o'clock in the morning. It was the sound of singing and it was coming from downstairs. Had she left her radio on? She knew she hadn't, so what was the singing? She got up and slowly walked downstairs and looked into her front room. She could not believe what she saw, for the six little fairies were dancing, flying about and singing. As she watched she just could not believe what she was seeing. Suddenly the fairies saw her and flew to the other side of the room. Mary said, "Don't be frightened, I won't harm you."

One little fairy said, "Hello, we were singing and dancing for we are so happy. Was it you who washed us?"

"Yes."

"Thank you, you have broken the spell that turned us into clay. What's your name?"

"I'm Mary." All the little fairies flew round her, each one saying, "Thank you Mary, thank you."

"What do you mean I broke the spell that was put on you?"

"I will tell you Mary."

"What are your names?" she asked, each little fairy in turn gave her name "I'm Teco,"

"Zeea,"

"Yanto,"

"Anco,"

"Byla,"

"Mota." Teco told Mary the story.

"We lived in Ireland a long time ago; our queen is Queen Bamboa, a wise and powerful but gentle beautiful queen who lived and looked over us. We lived in a small wood in fairy land, on the other side of the wood lived a King Gabins, he wanted to marry the queen but she did not want to marry him. He only wanted to marry so he could get her power for himself and rule all the fairies. Well one day he called on our queen and asked her to marry him, she again said no so he got very angry and said, "If you don't marry me I will put a spell on you all." But the queen said no, for her powers were much greater than his. "You will pay for turning me down." he told her. "I will put a spell on all your fairies so that when the sun goes down this day, every fairy that plays by the tiny rock will be turned into clay forever and a day."

"But the queen said, "Do what you will. I will break your spells." So she put a spell over her kingdom and the wood. She told all her fairies "No one is to leave her kingdom until the next sun comes up." She was told all the fairies were in her kingdom but what she did not know was six of us were playing at the tiny rock outside fairy land. Tiny rock is a small rock in a field outside MacGintey's woods; the queen's spell only covered the wood not the field. She thought she knew all her fairies were safe in her kingdom. King Gabins said to the queen "You have until sunset." again the queen said no so the king called out:

Rub a dub, dub all fairies in a tub,
Only soap and water my spell will alter,
And only a gentle hand release them from
Their prison land of clay
And heat from their head to their feet
A gentle hand will bring them back to fairy land.

"And when the sun went down we suddenly all turned to clay. When the queen found out she was very sad, a field mouse went and told her what had happened to us. The queen tried but could not break King Gabins' spell, so she made us into six clay teapots and put us out in the sun to dry, but a little girl walking through the wood found us and took us back to her home. We could hear everything our queen said but could not move or answer, so for many years we have been clay until you washed us."

"Thank you," All the little fairies called out "Thank you."

Mary said, "When will you go back to fairy land?"

"We will send a massage to our queen, for she can fly high and low, the wind will tell her all she wants to know. We will ask the wind to tell her of us and that we are free. She will send the bluebirds to take us back to fairy land but we will stay with you for three days, then we must go home." So for the next three days Mary had lots of fun with the fairies, she had grown to love them all very much.

Then it was time to go back to fairy land for the bluebirds were waiting for them. Zeea said "Our queen has sent you a message saying thank you for saving us and giving us our lives back. She has granted you one wish, anything you want," but Mary turned down their queen's offer, saying "I'm just happy that you can all go back to fairy land."

Byla said, "If you ever need our help when you hear the cuckoo call, call us and we will come to you." As they jumped on the backs of the bluebirds they called out, "Goodbye, goodbye Mary. We love you. Thank you for making us fairies again. Goodbye." Then the six bluebirds flew away back to fairy land, far across the sea back to Ireland. For the next few weeks Mary was very sad, the fairies had made her promise not to tell anyone about them or what she had done. She could not even tell Mini her best friend.

King Gabin was not a good king, he was not liked by his people; they did not want him to be their king . He tricked his brother into letting him wear the royal ring that had many powers and as soon as he had it on his finger he turned his brother into a frog then made himself king. Now when Mary heard the story from the fairies she did not realise what she was saying for she said, "I wish I could turn King Gabin into a frog and his brother back into a king again." So it happened, for the spell could only be broken by a human, like the fairies' spell was broken by a human – Mary. So Mary's one wish was granted without her knowing.

The fairies told many, many stories of their queen; they said she could make trees grow tall or small; she can talk to the birds and bees, flowers and trees and even make people sneeze. With that all the little fairies laughed. The little people were not bad but just naughty, they would do lots of things to the birds and animals. Here are some or the things they would do: steal the squirrel's nuts and put them over the ant holes so the ants had to work hard to push them away from their ant holes. Cut threads on the spider's web so the spider could not catch his dinner, sit on the flower buds early in the morning so that the buds could not open, and when the frog would make his mating croak they would answer back so the frog thought he had found a mate and would spend all night looking for her. "We ride on butterflies, dragonflies, bees and bluebirds and even ladybirds."

The fairies said, "The Gabions fly on moths and wasps and after the Gabions had finished their naughty tricks on the birds and animals they would run off, and the poor birds: when they went to breakfast they could not find any worms for the Gabins would find them first and hide all the worms and the fairies would go round putting everything back in its place." Mary used to love listening to all the fairies' little stories, they told her many things. She learnt little fairy songs and would sing with them and learn little dances. For those three days Mary was so happy.

It was about a month later that Mini rang Mary and told her Boots the cat had died in his sleep. She was so upset that she cried many times, Mary tried hard to cheer her up but she just could not. "Do you want another cat?" Mary asked her.

"No, I don't want any more animals." Mary did not know what to do to help her friend get over losing her cat. She'd had Boots for nearly 12 years. Mary wondered if the little fairies could help her, so she listened out for the cuckoo and as soon as she heard it she called out, "Little Fairies please help me. Little Fairies please help me!" then she waited for them to come. But they did not come, three days later still no fairies. "Oh dear," she said "I was so hopping they could help me, never mind, perhaps they've got lots to do." It was about one o'clock in the morning when Mary heard singing, she went downstairs as fast as she could and looked in her front room, and there she saw the six little fairies singing and dancing and flying around the room. As soon as they saw her they rushed to her and they all started talking at once. Over the next two hours Mary learnt all about the fairies going home; the king turned into a frog and his brother turned back into a king. Yanto said, "Why are you so sad Mary?" She told them all about Mini's cat dying and how she had tried to cheer her up but could not do so, "I offered to buy her another cat but she said no."

"Don't worry, we will help you." The little fairies started talking to one another, Mary could not understand what they were saying. They looked at Mary and laughed, "Don't worry Mary it's only fairy talk. We must go now we have a plan."

"Our queen has told us you will only see us once more. Goodbye Mary, Goodbye, we love you." Then they were gone. Mary sat up for the rest of the night she just could not sleep. It was another week before anything happened. Mini rang, "Mary, Mary, Mary come round my house."

"What's wrong?"

"Nothing, just come round as quick as you can." When Mary got to Mini's house she was waiting for her. "Come into the kitchen. Look Mary." and there in a little box was a very small black and white kitten. "Where did you find him?"

"It's strange, I looked into the garden because it looked like rain and I've got washing drying, and I saw a fox."

"A Fox?"

"Yes, never seen one in my garden before, it was by the bushes. It just sat there looking at me, then looking at the bushes, so I went out into the garden to see what the fox was doing, and looking at and in the bush I saw something moving. It was this little kitten, I got him out of the bush and when I looked round the fox had gone."

"What are you going to do with the kitten? You don't want anymore cats do you? Shall we take him down to the pet shop?"

"Err no, not now, I'll do it tomorrow." That told Mary all she wanted to know. Mini picked up the little kitten, cuddling him. "What name have you given him?"

"I think I'll call him Pepper, for as soon as I picked him up he sneezed four times." Mary just shook her head.

On her way home Mary said, "Thank you little fairies for your help."

A few days later Pat rang, "Mum can you baby sit for the weekend – John wants me to go to France with him, he's got a meeting in Paris and it will be nice to be on our own?"

"Yes, I will." so on Friday Mary was at Pat's house and before she knew it, it was Monday and John and Pat were back from France. John said to Mary, "You know my boss Sir Paul Richard? They have named a rose after him, I've got a paper do you want to read it? There's a picture of Sir Paul on the front page."

"No, I've lost my reading glasses I've looked everywhere for them but I just can't find them." They looked everywhere but could not find them. "They were on the table, I went to the kitchen and when I came back in they were gone."

Mary looked at the photo of her old friend in the paper and without realising it, started to read about Sir Paul Richard. Then it hit her she was reading the newspaper without her glasses. "Pat, Pat!" she called out.

"What's up Mum?"

"I've just read the paper without my glasses. I'm always losing them or forgetting them when I go out." What a week for Mary! That night when she went to bed she heard someone knocking at her window, looking out she saw six little fairies waving to her "Goodbye Mary!" they called out as they flew away. To Mary it looked like they were sitting on a pair of glasses. Mary shook her head and said "I need to get my eyes tested."

Warriors of the Wind

In 1740, Master Aki Wang was born in a small province called Akita, he was named Aki after it. In 1742 Master Shima Choshi was born in a small village called Mito, Mito is a small village on the west coast, it was not till 1768 that the two men would meet, when they did meet it would be a battle.

Aki Wang was in a small town called Ayaba, in an eating house. He sat in a corner looking out into the street; unknown to Aki Wang in the other corner of the eating house sat Shimo Choshi also having a meal. Aki Wang had almost finished his meal when six men of the local gang came in, seeing Aki Wang, a stranger to the town, they went over to him and demanded money. Aki Wang told them to go away and leave him alone to finish his meal.

One of the gang drew a knife and went for Wang, but before the knife man had gone two steps he was sent flying across the room from a kick to the head. Seeing this the other five attacked but within a minute all five were lying on the floor injured or running out of the eating house.

Shimo Choshi sat and watched Aki Wang sort out the six men, after Aki Wang has finished his meal he sat for a while then got up to leave. At the same time Shimo Choshi got up to leave, he wanted to talk to Wang.

Outside the eating house twenty of the gang were waiting for Wang, he saw them and knew another fight was about to start.

He called out, "It takes 20 of you to fight one man."

Then he heard a voice. It said, "No, it takes 20 men to fight two men", and Shimo Choshi stood by Aki Wang. Again the fight did not last long, for the gang was no match for Wang and Choshi, and again many of the gang ran off, some lay on the ground hurt and in pain, three were killed by the swords of Wang and Choshi. They fought side by side that day, together they became a very dangerous and powerful force, and that day their friendship was sealed for life.

Over the next 32 years they travelled across Japan teaching and fighting for a living. Wang was a karate master and master of many weapons. Choshi was also a karate master, but of a different style, and a master of the sword.

Aki Wang and Shimo Choshi, when they were small boys, had heard many stories of a great wind that came when a true and honest samurai was about to die on the battle field, or on his deathbed, it was said it 'called' you, but the evil samurai it passed by. The evil samurai never heard the wind call his name. Many times over the years they talked of the great wind, the wind was called the Wind of Rest, the Wind of Peace, the Peace Wind, it had many names.

In 1800, they reached a small fishing village called Kobe. From 1776 to 1800 they travelled all over Japan and over the years together had built a very high reputation for fighting and teaching the arts, and they were asked many times to help get rid of gangs terrorising small villages, and for the cost of a bed and a meal they did it many times.

In the summer of 1801 Wang was 60 and Choshi was 59 years old when they arrived in Kobe, again this was a small fishing village overrun by a gang, and again it did not take long for Wang and Choshi to clear the gang from the village.

Ika Wang at 60 fell in love with a fisherman's daughter, and Shimo Choshi, 59, fell in love with a farmer's daughter. They both married and felt at their age it was time to stop travelling and live the rest of their lives in Kobe. To make a living they could teach the arts, so for the next nine years that's what they did.

Ika Wang's wife had a daughter, they called her Lia, and Shimo Choshi's wife had two sons, one son was called Ika after his friend and the other son was called Mito after his home town.

In 1807 a pirate fishing gang tried to steal boats, nets, food and young girls from the village.

Wang, Choshi and some of their students took on the fishing pirates and after a very hard battle where many died, the pirates finally fled. Choshi was badly injured taking on seven pirates, it was only because of his age that they beat him, for the years of fighting and living rough had started to take their toll.

Choshi was ill for a very long time, it was only through the love of his family and the villages that looked after him day and night that Choshi finally got well again.

Wang and Choshi had built a dojo, it had four posts and a roof made of bamboo and straw, and under the roof Wang and Choshi trained their students. Now a strange thing used to happen but only when Choshi was in the dojo on his own, he used to say, "I can feel the wind blowing through the dojo, I can hear voices but can't make out what they are saying." This went on almost right through the year of 1809.

At the start of October of 1809 Wang and Choshi were teaching when Choshi fell to the ground, Wang rushed over to him, and held him in his arms. Choshi said, "Ika I'm dying, I can hear the wind calling to me, 'Come my samurai it's time to die'."

Then the wind started to blow through the dojo, it got stronger and stronger and in the air a strange noise could be heard. The wind was now so strong that Wang had to hold his friend very tight and bury his head against the very strong wind.

Then the great wind had gone, and so had Choshi, for while the great wind had blown through the dojo Choshi had died. No one in the village knew or felt the wind, only the students and Wang in the dojo. The dojo entrance faced the east and that was where the wind came from.

Wang decided to build a dojo in memory of his lost friend, calling it Spirit of the Wind, and put two styles together to make one style, calling the new style 'East Wind'.

Wang's daughter married one of her father's students, his name was Milshto. They had a son and called him Mito Milshto, after Chosh'si home town of Mito.

The East Wind

Of time there is none, of life there is some,
Of wind and rain they are the same,
But in death the east wind will call and cry,
And carry the soul of the dead Samurai,
A warrior in life is a warrior in death,
Yokomoto Agamioto Mishito
Ride the great wind,
Their eyes are on fire, their swords of steel,
They travel the wind as if on a great ferris wheel,
Their journey is endless and time is the same,
For the wind roars on, like chasing a flame.
The fallen warrior will hear the wind cry,
Come on my warrior it's time to die.
For the eyes of the living are dead to the wind,
The wind passes by the evil that die,
For only hell can hear them cry.
Many warriors ride the great wind,
They ride on chargers of white, black and grey,
But many great warriors run all the way,
I knew of a warrior who knew of a day,
The great east wind would carry him away.

Young Eagle

It was1850 and the great North American planes were so hot that nothing moved or wanted to, for it was mid-summer. Howling Wolfe, chief of the Qahatika, an Indian tribe had sent a small party of braves on a hunting trip.

The hunting party had just moved onto the planes when suddenly from nowhere a great North American eagle swooped down on them. The eagle was a bald eagle; a very large and powerful bird. As it swooped down on the hunting party it gave a screaming cry, it's talons out stretched as if it was going to attack, but it just flew off. It repeated this four times and then flew off and landed on a rock some 200 yards away from the hunting party.

The leader of the hunting party, Running Dog, said, "Let's kill the eagle and take it back to our people."

They had got about 100 yards from the eagle when it suddenly flew off and was not seen again. The hunting party was just about to turn back when they heard a crying sound coming from near the rock. Thinking it might be a young eagle, injured and that's why the mother eagle attacked them, they approached the rock.

Running Dog said, "The crying sound is like a young eagle calling its mother." When they got to where the crying was coming from, it was not a young eagle but a baby. It was a baby boy, Indian, about a few days old.

Where did the baby come from, and how did it get here they asked each other?

"We must return to our camp as quickly as possible," said Running Dog, "for the baby will not live long in this heat."

So they returned back to their camp as quickly as they could with the baby. When they told Howling Wolfe their story and gave him the baby he said, "I will call a counsel of the elders of the tribe."

It was agreed that the baby would become Howling Wolfe's son, for Howling Wolfe's wife had died giving him a son and then a few days later his son died, this was in the winter of 1850.

Howling Wolfe said, "I have listened to your story of the great eagle and of the baby, I shall name my son Young Eagle." So Young Eagle became the son of Howling Wolfe, chief of the Qahatika tribe.

From the very beginning Howling Wolfe felt that his new son was something special, but did not know how. Young Eagle had no fear of animals or of birds; by the time he was three years old he would run and play with the dogs on the camp, walk amongst the horses in the camp corral, he just had no fear.

By age five he would wander off and they would have to go out and find him, he was found many times sleeping in a wolf's den, but they never hurt him. He would sit and watch the young rabbits play, they would run and play by him they were not afraid of him. Many stories were told of him and the wild animals he played with.

He learnt very quickly the skills he had to learn, for Howling Wolfe had told him, "One day my son you will be chief of the Qahatika people, you must rule good and true and be a great warrior, for one day I must leave and go to the great hunting ground where my father and my father's father have gone before."

When Young Eagle was ten years old he went out hunting on his own, it was late in the afternoon and he had not found anything to kill to take back with him. He came to a small stream and, he started to drink from it he saw the face of an Indian chief looking out at him from the water. The chief was in full headgear; he spoke to Young Eagle, saying, "Listen well, for I speak naught but words of truth, for the Great Spirits of the Mountains and of the Great Planes have chosen you to be given the powers of life and death. You are given this day three lives which you can give to other people, to animals, or birds when death is near, or keep for yourself, you must call out these words:

Great Spirits of the sky, mountains and the Great Planes,
Hear me this day.
For I am Young Eagle
Give one of my lives to…

"Farewell my young warrior." Then the spirit was gone.

Young Eagle started to return to his camp, when he heard a crying sound coming from a hole in the ground near an old fallen tree, looking down into the hole he saw a young baby eagle, it was looking up at him crying. It took a long time to get to the baby eagle but at last he got the eagle out, it was a bald eagle, about one month old. Its wing was cut and it had lost a lot of blood from a wound in its side.

Young Eagle spent many hours looking after the baby eagle, Mossa, meaning 'sky friend'. Also spelt Mosa, meaning 'Eyes in the sky, eyes of the heavens', Mossa., or Mosa, had many Indian meanings.

Howling Wolfe said, "You have chosen well the name for your feathered friend".

Very slowly the small bird started to get well and stronger and started to grow. The young eagle would look at Young Eagle and cry out, Young Eagle would look at his small bird friend and then go off to catch fish and other food, for he instinctively knew what his friend wanted.

Howling Wolfe asked his son, "Can you understand what the baby eagle is saying?" But Young Eagle would never answer, he just laughed and ran off.

Young Eagle was loved by the tribe, the young boys and girls of his age used to laugh at him and his eagle and play games on him, but he just laughed and they would run off with him and play.

There were many stories told about Young Eagle and his eagle, it was said that Young Eagle could talk to his eagle. One such story was that Young Eagle went to Howling Wolfe and said, "The cavalry is riding to the camp, there are many soldiers with guns, they are coming to kill us and burn down our camp, we must go up into the hill until they have gone".

So Howling Wolfe called his people together and told them of the soldiers coming, "We must leave now." Howling Wolfe led his people up into the hills and soon the soldiers came and burnt down everything in the camp then left.

"You have this day saved your people." Howling Wolfe told Young Eagle.

Wherever Young Eagle went, Mosa would fly above him crying out and Young Eagle would raise his arm as if he was answering back, saying "Thank you, my friend."

Another story about Young Eagle, is that when out with six other young braves, Mosa was flying high up in the sky, when suddenly it swooped down, crying out to Young Eagle. Young Eagle stopped and said, "There are soldiers ahead ready to ambush us, we must turn back."

Four of the braves laughed at him and said, "Your eagle told you that?" and rode off.

The other two braves turned back with Young Eagle, some time later they heard gunfire coming from where Young Eagle had said where the ambush would be.

At the camp they told Howling Wolfe, Howling Wolfe sent a large party of braves to find and bring back the four dead braves. They were all found shot dead by the soldiers' guns.

Howling Wolfe asked Young Eagle, "How did you know of the ambush?"

"My eagle told me, for I can understand his calls and cries."

When Young Eagle was 13, he was sent out hunting with Mosa, who was flying in front of him, when a shot rang out and Mosa fell to the ground. Young Eagle ran to him but Mosa was dead. Young Eagle held his friend in his arms and wept, he had great pain in his heart and for many hours Young Eagle wept more and he held his friend in his arms. As the sun started to set he called out, "Great Spirits of the sky, the mountains and the Great Planes, hear me this day, for I am Young Eagle. Give one of my lives to my friend Mosa the great eagle".

But the eagle, Mosa, lay in his arms and did not move and did not come back to life. After many more hours Young Eagle buried his great lost friend, then he set out to kill the person who killed his beloved eagle.

He found a white hunter not far away and left him for dead, then he returned to his camp. He told Howling Wolfe of the death of his eagle and the killing of the white hunter.

Howling Wolfe said, "My son you will find another great eagle and again your friend will fly the great skies".

But the following morning as the sun broke the sky, a great cry rang out, Young Eagle ran from his bed and there circling above him was Mosa. Young Eagle cried with joy, laughed and in tears, he hugged his father, and called, "Mosa, Mosa, Mosa!" and Mosa called back from the skies.

Young Eagle left his camp and was not seen for many days, for it was said he and Mosa went into the mountains.

About 15 miles from Howling Wolfe's camp was another tribe of Indians called Jicarilla.

There was a young girl Young Eagle had fallen in love with called Lyesha, she was also in love with Young Eagle. Also there was a young brave who loved Lyesha and asked her to marry him, but she had turned him down saying, "My heart has been taken by Young Eagle of the Qahatika, for soon our blood will be of one."

The Jicarilla were great hunters and did not get on with the Qahatika because they would hunt very near to the Qahatika camp.

Young Eagle was now 16 years old and Mosa had been with Young Eagle for 10 years. Bald eagles can live for 30 years and are almost fully grown by 13 weeks. They are fed up to 20 weeks old and are almost forced out of the nest by their parents and left to fend for themselves, but sorry to say only about half live. They make a screaming crying noise as they fly high in the sky. The bald eagle is a North American eagle.

One hunting party led by Broken Lance, the young brave who loved and wanted to marry Lyesha, was only a few miles from the Qahatika camp when he saw this eagle following them and crying out from the sky. Broken Lance knew that the eagle was Young Eagle's eagle and made plans with his other braves to kill it, to get back at Young Eagle. He wanted Young Eagle and the eagle dead, for his heart carried bad blood.

"When the eagle is overhead our arrows must find the eagle's heart." But the eagle would not fly low or near Broken Lance's hunting party. "Let's ride to the mountains and wait for the eagle, we will hide in the rocks, it will come to look for us, and we can kill it then".

So to the mountains they went, the eagle followed but did not see one of the braves hiding in the rock, and as the eagle flew over an arrow hit him. The eagle fell from the sky and fell down the side of a cliff, it was a high cliff and steep. Unknown to Broken Lance, Young Eagle had followed and had seen the eagle shot down by an arrow and fall below the cliff edge.

After Broken Lance's party left, Young Eagle tried to get down the cliff to get to his friend Mosa, but it was no use. Again his beloved eagle had been killed, so Young Eagle called out to the spirits, "Great Spirits of the Skies and of the Mountains and the Great Planes, hear me this day for I am Young Eagle, give one of my lives to Mosa the great eagle."

Then he returned back to his camp to await the new day and for his faithful friend to return from the dead. Unknown to Young Eagle his friend was not dead, so when a few days later the great eagle cried out above Young Eagle's bed, Young Eagle thought the sprits had given his eagle's life back and he had used two lives up to save his friend.

It was nearly three years later when Young Eagle was 18 years old that Broken Lance was to seek ever lasting revenge on Young Eagle. He planned to kidnap Lyesha and take her to Canada, but he was told that Lyesha was pregnant. Broken Lance did not know these words were told to him by his mother.

"For this," he told his friends, "they both must die, I will poison her drinking water and with a soldier's gun I will kill Young Eagle, for if I cannot hold Lyesha in my arms, Young Eagle will not".

So late at night he poisoned Lyesha's drinking water, Lyesha drank the water and fell dying. They called Young Eagle and told him Lyesha had been poisoned by drinking the water. Her dog also drank the water and was dead, and it would not be long before Lyesha would also die.

Young Eagle held Lyesha in his arms and wept many tears, Young Eagle looked up from Lyesha and standing in front of him was Broken Lance with a soldier's gun in his hand.

"You have given me many years of pain, taking my Lyesha away from me, now I have taken her away from you and again I will be taking, but this time I will be taking your life." and at that he fired at Young Eagle, two shots, both hitting him in the chest.

As Young Eagle lay dying he called out to the spirits, "Great Spirits of the skies and of the Mountains and of the Great Planes, give one of my lives to Lyesha so that she may live once more."

Soon afterwards Young Eagle died, and as the full moon started to greet the day, Lyesha opened her eyes and lived. Six months later she gave birth to a baby boy.

What Young Eagle did not know was that when Mosa was hit by the arrow it went through part of his wing so that he could not fly, and so fell down the cliff, but by doing so the arrow was pulled out of his wing and for 2 days, Mosa lay on the edge of the cliff but was able to get back into the air, (we don't know how, maybe the spirits helped him). Young Eagle had used two lives both on Mosa, and one life on Lyesha, making three lives all used up .He died not knowing he had one life left, by saving Lyesha her baby also lived, using his last life on his Lyesha.

He said, "If I had one more life I would give to my unborn baby instead of taking the life for myself." But at the birth of her son, Lyesha died. As Lyesha died a great heavy mist came down and high in the sky you could hear but not see, the cry of the great North American bald eagle, then the cry was gone and so was the son of Young Eagle.

It was the year of 1874, Young Eagle had only lived for 24 years, the baby was never found nor was the eagle seen again.

On the borders of America and Canada was an Indian tribe called Saulteaux. A hunting party from the Saulteaux tribe was heading towards the Canadian boarder when suddenly from nowhere a great North American eagle swooped down. For the end is the beginning.

POINTS OF INTEREST

The American eagle (bald eagle) comes from North America to Mexico and lives for about 30 years.
The American eagle is fully grown in about 13 weeks but its parents still supply it with food for about 20 weeks.
The baby eagle is called an eaglet.
It has a screaming cry as it flies the skies.

TRIBES

There was, between 1850-1874 and on, Indian tribes called:
Jicarillav
Navaho
Mohave
Qahatika

These tribes lived in the north of the U.S.A.
Near the U.S.A. and Canadian border other tribes on and around the border were called:
Saulteaux
Blood
Blackfoot
Peigan
Sarcee
Stoney
Chipewyan.